Vibrator

Vibrator

First published in Japan in 1999 by Kondansha Ltd.

First published in Great Britain in 2005 by Faber and Faber

©Mari Akasaka, 1999

Translation © Michael Emmerich, 2005

ISBN-13: 978-1-933368-61-0

Published by Soft Skull Press

55 Washington St., Suite 804

Brooklyn, NY 11201

Cover Design by Gary Fogelson

Cover Art by Laurie Simmons

Interior Design by Anne Horowitz

Distributed by Publishers Group West

www.pgw.com 1-800-788-3123

Library of Congress Cataloging-in-Publication Data

Akasaka, Mari.

 [Vaibureta. English]

 Vibrator / by Mari Akasaka ; translated from the Japanese by
Michael
Emmerich.

        p. cm.

 ISBN-13: 978-1-933368-61-0 (alk. paper)

 ISBN-10: 1-933368-61-6 (alk. paper)

 I. Emmerich, Michael. II. Title.

PL845.K328V3513 2007

895.6'36--dc22

2006100985

Vibrator

by

Mari Akasaka

Translated from the Japanese by Michael Emmerich

Soft Skull Press / Brooklyn, New York / 2007

Drop dead, you old bastard.

Yeah, you too, girl—you get it.

The voices were really getting on my nerves.

Why the fuck didn't you say something why'd you fucking freeze up like that why the hell didn't you counterattack huh you know those bastards are harmful right you know they've gotta be eliminated?

Spiraling through my head, my own thoughts harass me. Hey I'm not like that I can't afford to screw around when you're in my position you gotta act your age. A lame attempt to protest. Then all at once the words stop coming, my thoughts have broken off. And in the pause I hear a voice beyond my control:

Gotta act your rage?

Without thinking, I glanced around. The words sounded like the ones I'd just spoken; it was the same pathetic excuse—"You gotta act your age"—but the voice was different. And I knew right away that *this* voice was saying "act your rage," not "act your age." Ha ha, yeah, that's great. You wanna turn

rage into action, your blood's boiling and you're
dying to turn up the heat, you want it to boil over,
isn't that it? Isn't that it, huh? I'm telling you, girl,
you were ready to explode! You should have made
mincemeat of that old bastard, him and the damn
girl, too. You've got enough strength for that, right?
You're no fool. You get worried that you might lose
your job and shit, but you know what? All that
shows is that you lack confidence, it's as simple as
that . . . All that crap about not wanting to ruin the
atmosphere, don't give me that, don't try to push the
blame onto others.

This was the first time I'd ever heard a voice
beyond my control when there were so many people
around, and I came dangerously close to screaming.

"Oh yeah . . . I wanted to get some wine. That's
what I came here for . . ." I said, quietly speaking
the words in an effort to get back into my own
thoughts. And then suddenly I started setting
words to music, singing. White, white wine, white,
white wine, not very mu-uch like French wine . . .
Can't stand those acidic ones, *non, non, non!* Reality
had returned, at least a little. Why is it that they
don't make red wine in Germany? I considered the
matter. But that triggered things: it started up
again. What do you mean, there are some—aren't
there? Nope, they're white, they're whi-ite, over-
whelming-ly whi-ite, Madonna, Madonna, delicious
Madonna, why is it that there are no red wines in
Germany?

Here they go again, starting in on me with their chitter-chatter. Starting inside me. Chitter-chatter-chitter-chatter-chitter-chatter-chitter-chatter. And to make matters worse, this time the chitter-chatter-chitter-chatter is stuck in a loop.

Finally I just couldn't take it anymore and yelled out—

Look, would you just *shut the fuck up*!

But maybe I wasn't shouting, just struggling, struggling with all my might to hold it in . . . Either way, the voices quieted down, and the inside of my head became *absolutely still*. Without thinking, I glanced around. A convenience store in the dead of night, no different from any other. Today is March 14: White Day! One Month After Valentine's Day, When You Give Him Your Heart, Will Your Darling Give You His in Return? Today's the Day Men Live Up to Their Women's Love! Man, I've gotta watch myself. OK, I guess I didn't actually say anything. Give me a fucking break, I groan bitterly to myself. I hope none of you assholes are actually being fooled by these Mechanical Passion Apparatuses. No one paid the slightest attention to me, for better or for worse. Smart Families Start at Family Mart. I'm not acting strange. Not getting any strange looks. Everything's OK. I've just got too many thoughts in my head, that's all, I wonder how I look to people. Normal, I guess: an office worker heading home late after a night on the town? No, no, the clothes are too flashy for an office worker. I'm telling you, this girl's a

little bit stra-ange! Nah, I'm being too self-conscious,
that's all—that's all. Taking revenge on yourself
'cause you didn't have the guts to do what you felt
like doing? The *me* that should have acted instead of
letting them argue *me* down; the *me* that should have
resisted—it's all streaming out now, turning into
sentences? Come on, it happens all the time. I see
my opponent's weak spot afterwards—the point that
would've made him crumble if only I'd had the
sense to hit him there. It only comes to me later.
That's what always happens. I'm always too slow to
understand.

So is that why you write?

The voice was back. A voice that was male, sexless,
composite—inorganic.

Don't ask that question! I shake my head, trying
to shake the voice. Don't ask me those fundamental
questions. Don't ask me—just don't ask. Hell, I don't
even know who you are. I have no words of my own.
I can't write words of my own. Is it my work? Have I
just heard too many stories from too many people? I
have nothing, nothing at all. So I wanted to fill the
void with their feelings.

A sense of powerlessness began pressing down
on me, weighing so heavily on my shoulders that I
nearly crumpled to the floor. I'd just blabbed the one
answer I really, really didn't want to know anything
about.

Please, please stop—(a voice weaker than any of
the rest that have appeared until now, a sort of mur-

mur, interjects, pleading; voices completely out of my control tend to come bubbling up when I'm feeling the most tense, or when I'm really exhausted) — fighting, the voice says, so weakly it seems right on the point of expiring. I have no idea whose voice it is: it seems like a voice I once knew, long ago; the kind of voice you would get if you took everything that exists in this world and spun it all together, compressing it all into a single, thin line — and it seems to rise up from somewhere like an air-hole in the weakened, worn-down barrier that encircles my self.

I feel such tenderness for this thing pleading inside me, begging the voices to stop, please stop; my heart ached for it; I wanted to treasure this thing that surfaced in an effort to protect me. But deep inside there's a latent rage that overpowers the tenderness; I can feel this rage shooting through me, piercing me, vertically, from head to foot. Everything I see, I'll send it all flying — fucking die, all of you! Drop dead, you old bastard, you and the girl, too! And you and you and you! It's your fault I'm suffering so horribly, right? You're the ones who are trying to corner me! The *me* who wants to fold herself in her own arms and the *me* who wants to attack everything around her . . . both of them, they're both me . . . and so I just stood there, motionless.

"Oh yeah . . . I wanted to get some wine, that's what I came here for . . ." I said again, as if I'd only just noticed. A teenage guy turned to look at me.

I had come to this store so often that I had the schedule down pat: I knew which workers were here at which times, when their shifts ended and everything. I came here from home all the time. This was the only store around that had all the things I wanted at night. Specifically: assorted processed foods, soda and alcohol. When did that begin, I wonder? . . . The voices inside me that do the thinking got so annoyingly loud they made it impossible for me to sleep. Usually they were my own thoughts, but then every so often some of the talk I'd heard from people while I was out doing interviews would appear, mixed in with the rest, and then I could respond to their questions according to my own sense of what was right; the scenes would play themselves out just as I'd wanted them to—those times when I really wanted to tell the person how much her or his story had moved me, or when I was yearning to tell some asshole to quit fucking around, but instead of coming out and saying these things I'd tried to make myself seem perfectly objective or to build up the person, keeping my own urges in check.

The voices were either my own or ones I'd heard—every one of them. Once in a while I might hear something the mother of a friend from my elementary-school days had said, stuff like that, perfectly true resurrections of memories that came from nowhere, or so it seemed, taking me by surprise, but there were no voices I hadn't actually encountered at some point in the past.

After a while I figured out a trick. I realized that booze helped me to sleep, because when I drank the number of voices would decrease. A gap would appear between one response and the next, and then one by one, one by one, the voices would disappear, and I would drop into a deep pool of peaceful sleep.

But my true honeymoon with alcohol was all too brief.

There are certain times when it's settled from the outset: once you start drinking, you're bound to end up going on a binge; drink has no lower limit. I'm not really doing it to sleep; I want to feel that there's nothing in the world but me and booze. I stop caring about tomorrow: the whole world *is* just me and booze. I feel omnipotent. I feel myself expanding, and ideas for new articles start streaming up inside me, one after the other. It feels so great I can hardly contain myself. And then, say someone phones me or something, I hate the idea of lessening the pleasure I feel, of spoiling the mood even a little, so even if I feel the urge to pee I don't tell the person, I don't put the caller on hold. Because I just can't stand how it feels when you come back from the bathroom and discover that the conversation has already ended for the person you were just talking to, and the chances are that it's already left you, too, and you realize that even if you were to work really hard to try to recoup that pleasure, it's gone, the mood has passed and it isn't going to return. I can't stand that feeling, I really can't. So one time I reached out and grabbed an empty coffee jar and a mug and then one of those giant cups they give you at sushi bars, every container within reach that happened to catch my eye, and let the urine flow while I talked, the receiver still in my hand. I was amazed to see how much the human bladder holds—it was so much more than I'd thought. More than the jar could contain, enough to fill the mug to the brim and then the cup after that, and there was still a little left.

Frantically, I emptied my pen-holder, converted it into a receptacle.

And then, finally, I was done.

Mornings after nights like that, I wake up mired in a despair as heavy as lead. The room is in such a disastrous state, it's really not something you want to see in the daylight. That sense of despair, my body so weighed down it seems completely clogged with waste, right down to my nerve endings—I have to get away. So, without even thinking, I toss down another gin. Experiences like this just keep repeating themselves; they never accumulate. How long can it go on? But when something new comes up and I have to rush out and get started on a new assignment, there's a kind of core in me that rises up out of inebriation, and the feeling I get then makes me think I'm a girl who can get things done, and I like it.

The second trick I learned was self-induced vomiting. It happened around the time I started getting flabby from the drinking, so I was able to kill two birds with one stone. I went to interview a girl with an eating disorder and I had a revelation. I've got bulimarexia, she said. Bulimarexia? If you refuse food, if you don't eat, you've got anorexia. If you eat way too much, you've got bulimia. And if you go on binges and then throw it all up, if you're doing what people refer to as self-induced vomiting, then you've got bulimarexia. It's a word they made up for people in the middle, see? Except now people just call it bulimia. That's the one I've got—that's me. Do you have any idea what might have brought it on? I asked her, speaking just fast enough to keep her from putting up her guard. I got the feeling she would just keep repeating the same thing, nothing but I'm bulimarexic, I'm bulimarexic! over and over again if I didn't make her stop. Her legs were so emaciated you could look between them and see what was on the other side; you could see how distorted her bones were and how her joints hooked up; you could see it all, and yet the girl had on a mini-skirt. I just didn't understand her sense of beauty. Girls with disorders, people say we want to have a copy of the Statue of Liberty with our own face on it erected in Tokyo bay. That's what they say. They say we go around thinking: I'm number one in the entire world! And that is what we want to be, see, number one. But if no one's going to pay attention to you anyway, you're much better off being sick. And besides, she went on, when you've got bulimarexia—

You sleep really well.

I stared at her.

In the beginning, when I first started experimenting with self-induced vomiting, I felt a lot of fear. I had to keep telling myself that life is all about new experiences. The first time was painful, because I'd never had the experience of vomiting up solids; not intentionally, anyway. But that night, strange as it seems, I really did sleep well; extremely well. As peacefully as a baby cradled in its mother's arms. I started poring over various books about eating disorders. And so I learned. Vomiting puts too much stress on the human body, so a flood of endorphins is released to soften the effects—that's how it works. Self-induced vomiting is tasty three times over: it's good while you're eating; it's good that you throw up and lose weight; and it's good because you sleep like a log. This wasn't something I happened upon experientially—I only ventured into the realm of experience after I'd done a bit of research into the mechanism behind it—so in a sense my behavior was quite logical. When I conducted these little experiments, everything was under my supervision. So I figured I could control myself completely.

Except there was a catch: I started to enjoy throwing up. I didn't want to waste the food I'd eaten: I was always eating things I wanted to eat, savoring the flavors, but when it came to resisting that pleasure, I was helpless. The profound sense of calm you feel when you've finished vomiting isn't the sort of thing you ever encounter naturally; it just doesn't happen. Imagine it . . . you can enjoy this feeling without using any chemicals, using nothing but substances already found in your body! It was like magic—a special, magical dietary program; a kind of alchemy that took place within my body; one hundred and ten pounds of flesh, pure flesh, nothing else. I discovered that when it came to throwing up, I was a total genius. I'd drink, then when I started feeling sick I would trot off to the bathroom and do some quick vomiting and right away I'd be back in action, able to start drinking again. Maybe I'd had this ability from the start; was that it? It's the sort of talent only certain people have; and if you don't have it, you'll never get it. For better or for worse, I had it. So, whenever my body started feeling sick before my brain had finished, when my head was screaming for more, or on nights when I'd been drinking gallons even though I had an important job the next day, then I would always vomit. And the next morning I'd set out for work, feeling great. At times like that, I felt like a winner.

In a man's world, it's easier to get by as a woman like this.

The problem with my calculations was that I'd failed to realize vomiting alcohol and vomiting food are two entirely different things. People first started drinking alcohol for pleasure—it had festive connotations—so if you stop letting alcohol be absorbed into your body, it's totally different from refusing to take in food. Stupid as it seems, I hadn't grasped that concept at all. Once the food starts getting mixed up with your stomach acids, vomiting becomes painful. So you've got to aim for just the right time, before this happens, and drink something—clear, fizzy drinks are best, I find. (For some reason, Coke is too intense, maybe because of the odor, or because some of the ingredients are stimulants; I don't know.) At any rate, you let this liquid, soda water, for example, turn the solid food into a fluid of precisely the right consistency, a sort of gel, and then all at once you throw it up. Tears flood your eyes when it happens. Is it because you're sad, because you find it all so pathetic, or is it a simple physiological reaction that is accompanied by no emotion at all, like the tears of the sea turtle laying her eggs? I don't know. But once I've given myself over to these tears, they can't be stopped. Then I begin to shake—a trembling that was hidden deep down inside me rises to the surface along with saline solution spilling from my eyes—and the shaking won't stop, either. Once I start leaking this salty fluid, everything inside me gets sucked out. Of course, I still have no idea why I'm crying, whether it's some kind of osmosis or whatever, or whether it really is all in my head, I have no idea, but I continue to cry, and sometimes I suck my fingers. Then, like a child, I drift off to sleep.

My skin started looking really bad. If my hand slipped and I cut myself with a knife or something, it took noticeably longer for the wound to heal. The cut would remain there for ages, the skin hard and purple. It reached the point where my fingernails were nearly always split, peeling apart into two layers, because I was no longer able to absorb as much nutrition as I needed.

Nevertheless, I did sleep well. The annoying tumult of thought that had always been pestering me until I tumbled down into sleep had completely disappeared. Except that some time around then I started hearing the voices that were beyond my control. One night, having completed the usual routine—a series of actions that had now become ceremonial—just as I was about to entrust myself to the embrace of a deep and restful sleep, the last remaining shred of my consciousness started wondering if I had turned off the gas. The question became a voice I had never heard before, and the voice kept echoing through my head. That was a *very* eerie experience. So even when I flicked off my thoughts again and tried as hard as I could to fall asleep, my brain started thinking again. I needed to know that the thoughts flowing through my head sounded like my own voice. I was confused.

Even then I didn't stop vomiting.

Maybe because I'd already digested my dinner past the point where I could barf it up—maybe that was why I came here. Meandering aimlessly through the overly bright interior of Family Mart, I thought:

No, no, that's not it, I wanted to go to a club. Yeah, I remember now, I figured I wouldn't be able to get sleep tonight anyway so I wanted to go to a club. But the club I had in mind was closed. My face was looking a little better, so I took off my sunglasses and put in contacts instead. I remember going pretty heavy on the makeup around my eyes—where was I when I did that? The memory is gone. The bathroom of some video arcade somewhere . . . maybe. I have no recollection of that, none at all. I never vomit digested food, so it had been settled from the start even while I was eating—there would be no vomiting tonight. By the time food has started dissolving into your gastric juices, it gets so painful to vomit that it's like having the pit of your stomach put through a ringer, and the acid eats away at your teeth and at the mucus in your esophagus. I ate tons of food today. When you're eating with people you don't really get along with, you get so damn bored that you end up eating too much, drinking too much. I wonder if this is how chain smokers feel when they get compulsive about their smoking. Man, I should have just told them no when we reached the end of that dismal panel discussion and started talking about going out to eat. That's what I should have done, but instead I went along; though, to tell the truth, I was feeling totally wasted, totally, so beat I reckoned if I didn't get something to eat I wouldn't be able to walk. I have to say, you certainly took your sweet time, considering you were with such assholes; you were eating pretty damn carefully, huh? Serving yourself from the lazy Susan, taking shrimp, crab, greens, fried noodles, noodles in broth—all foods I'm wild about, but I wasn't tasting the flavors at all. Come to think of it, I drank an entire bottle of laochu almost entirely on my own. Even then my skin never lost that hyper-sensitive feel, so I developed an urge to let my body be rocked by waves of very, very loud music. When you're in a club it's OK to slam into other people.

The first time you ram into someone, you hit them with your anger. You feel rage in the pain of the collision. Then, without waiting, you go and crash into a second person and then a third, a fourth, a fifth, bashing into them with different parts of your body, and then you feel rage start to dissolve in the lingering traces of pain: it's taken apart, broken down into separate elements of something that isn't anger anymore; you feel your body being enveloped within something like a membrane of frozen, numbed exhaustion. The impulse towards collision at acute angles subsides now, and instead of colliding you start to writhe, stretching out a rapid hand to brush parts of bodies of people nearby; you rub against people. As if to pickpocket pieces of them. A rush of erotic feeling surges up inside you. You start to feel grateful that you're living like this, not just letting your rage take control. At times like these you want to be in a really huge place with a really great sound system. The kind of place that gets so packed that it looks like a bucket of potatoes when you see it from above. At clubs there's never any pause between one song and the next. That's not surprising, but it's still very important. Somewhere out there the beat is always throbbing, the beat is always throbbing within you, somewhere inside your body, you're completely passive in the grip of the sound; it feels like you're not even there. It feels like you're not even you.

I want to touch someone. If it's too hard to start touching, then I want a reason to touch. I'm frightened of people I can't touch, I'm frightened of people whose skin I can't cover with my own, ever so gently, two surfaces together. I feel as if I'm about to be attacked, and so I feel as if I'm about to attack. I worry that I might act too aggressively in self-defense; I might lash out and suddenly kill them . . .

Why the fuck did I agree to take part in such a crappy panel?

I kept cursing quietly to myself as I wandered up and down the merchandise-lined aisles of Family Mart, doing nothing. Did it please me to think I'd become a bigger name—was that why I liked being referred to as a "journalist" now, when in the past I'd just been a "reporter"? Did I think in the long run it would be good for me to step into the limelight now? I used to go around ringing the doorbells of people who had suffered some kind of tragedy—I'd stand there asking the relatives, "Can you tell me how it

feels?"—that's the kind of work I was doing, but
then I started dealing with issues like high school
prostitutes (call them what you like, they're still
prostitutes) and AIDS and junkies and the homeless
and aid for the homeless and juvenile drug dealers
and organ transplants and brain death, the pros and
cons of cloning. And when I started dealing with
that stuff, approaching it all from my own particular
perspective, my name started attracting the attention
of a particular crowd. Yeah, and then one day it
happened, it crashed down over me like thunder,
like the revelations I used to have when I was
drinking, and I thought: This is it, girl, this is the
major break you've been waiting for! I had been
invited to participate in a panel discussion by a well-
known women's magazine.

The topic under discussion was "What Makes
Teenage Boys Snap?" Young males, particularly guys
in junior high school, had been committing murders
and other violent crimes fairly regularly in the wake
of a brutal killing and other attacks carried out by a
fourteen-year-old from Kobe—crimes that gave the
distinct impression that they were intended to convey some kind of message. For a women's fashion
magazine to be putting together a special issue on a
subject like this, either the topic had to be really hot
or the magazine had to be really short on ideas for
feature articles. This magazine usually used photographers known for doing a good job with people.
Since I was sort of involved with mass media myself,

I knew that. The thing is, there are photographers who work well with objects, and photographers who work well with people, and the magazine uses them accordingly. So the guys who take pictures of people are the guys who take good pictures of people. Right. But even so, three days before the panel, I had already decided that I needed to look as good as possible in the photos. I would definitely have to give up vomiting, that was for sure, because it shows in your skin. But as soon as I started thinking like that, the stress of being strictly forbidden to vomit kept me awake at night, so I took to drinking cocktails of sleeping pills and booze and my face became all puffy.

I have to look good for the camera.

Not too many options were available to me in terms of strategy. I decided to go with the image of the eccentric who doesn't really like making appearances of this sort but is able to think on her feet once she's in a heated discussion. My eyes were so swollen and they had such huge bags under them that I had no choice but to cover them with a pair of light purple sunglasses, so I made these the core around which I coordinated my entire outfit. My perm was starting to grow out, but I did a good job curling my hair and made it spiral like it had in the beginning, and I wore a hat to keep readers from being distracted by my skin. My hair had a lot of body, and the way it fanned out under the edge of my tight hat was just perfect, the balance was exactly right—even I was impressed. Listen, say what you like, this is a fashion magazine we're talking about here.

You have to wonder what they had in mind when they selected the participants, though. A fifty-something university professor whose field was philosophy; some television personality who had just turned twenty; and me. These were the three faces that came together that day: one guy who's able to look at the big picture, a girl who's almost the same age as the kids in question, and one woman who believes in going to the scene. I could see what they were aiming for by bringing us together, but somehow it gave me a bad feeling. The editor was a pretty woman in her late twenties who didn't seem very connected to everyday life; the photographer was a man in his twenties. He had a kid's face and a moustache.

Every time the photographer snapped a picture of me while I was talking, I'd lose my concentration and be unable to say anything that had any meaning whatsoever. I felt as if his gaze could penetrate my skin. Stop doing that, stop looking through me that way—that far. Don't look at my heart. Use a strobe to make my face seem smoother; my skin looks so terrible, the epidermis is totally desiccated, all this is going to show up just as it is in real life, just as rough. Don't take my picture in natural light. Use a strobe, make me look good. Actually, my skin is so rough it might diffuse more light. Who knows, maybe it'll make my skin tone appear more even. I heard the snap of the shutter. When I have to keep worrying about having my picture taken like this, it feels as if some large fraction of my nerves are being physically torn out of my body. I'm not imagining it—I stop being able to focus. All the little bumps on my skin break themselves down into smaller bumps; I start to feel the surface of my body is the entire world. So, as the differential becomes smaller and smaller, as the unit of measurement decreases, the integral, which is to say my surface area, increases—is that how it goes? Wow, I get it! All of a sudden I felt like slapping my knee: for the first time in my life, I understood differentials and integrals. A flash of light sliced through my head. And then, just as I realized that this really wasn't the right time to be thinking about such things—

"And what's your view?"

The ball has been tossed back into my court. The camera turns my way. I get my face ready and hold it for a moment, then let it go and start talking.

"I think—"

Just an instant of motion, that's really all it is—a blurred instant as far as I'm concerned—that's what the camera responds to. No matter how hard I work to get the timing right, the finger that snaps the shutter responds only to the blur. The room has a nice feel to it—there's a huge window and it's bright, the afternoon is bright—so the cameraman refuses to shoot with anything but natural light. Hey, come on, I'm begging you here, would you please use a strobe, use a strobe to make the blemishes fade, and while you're at it, do me a favor and make my consciousness fade, too.

Will you use a *fucking flash*!

The photographer went on shooting with natural light.

"Sometimes, when you're out shopping or something, you start to feel cornered, you know, even though you're supposed to be having fun. Even after you buy something, the media still keep after you, keep trying to egg you on. 'Hey, it's time for a change! Product X will open up a whole new world of possibilities!' and so on. They keep after you until you start thinking that maybe this new product really is better. So the objects you buy start losing their appeal the moment you've bought them. Sometimes I just toss stuff aside when I get home without even bothering to open the bag. And ever since I was a teenager, every time people ask me how much something cost, I always tell them a price lower than it actually was. Because I just hate myself for having bought the thing. Where does this hatred come from? The ads and me, we're only acting according to principals of the market, right, and it seems to me that in contemporary society, the principal principles are those of the market. That's all I'm doing, just acting on the principles."

Shit. I've just blurted out a load of stuff that no one will follow unless they see it written down. Well, I suppose I can go over it in the galleys.

"And yet I get so exasperated I can hardly stand it. I go to the bank, and even though I'm making a perfectly legitimate withdrawal from my own account, that's all I'm doing, even so, I start having little alarms go off at me just because I've stood there a little too long without taking the banknotes. There's this beeper going off at me, beep-beep-beep-beep-beeping at me, it feels as though I'm being chastised, and I start to wonder why the hell I'm being chased away like this, you know, and before I know it I'm gritting my teeth or . . . . The point I'm trying to make is that we're totally surrounded by these stimuli, they're everywhere, it's enough to make a person neurotic, and just perceiving these things is enough to keep our nerves going, keep them firing as rapidly as they can manage. And, of course, as long as we go on living in modern society we have to keep trying to ignore these things, which means that we're constantly tricking our nervous systems. Trying to keep ourselves from feeling. So when the real alarms start going off—well, could it be that we just don't hear them? Even when the situation is really dangerous? Aren't there times like that, when you're in that sort of state, and some stupid little thing happens—something unexpected—and you get so terrified and your immediate reaction is to become overly defensive? It happens, right? Well, you know what it is? It means the nerves that are meant to respond to unexpected events are already working at full capacity. It happens to me. When I get really pissed off by the ATM, sometimes I'll go outside and I'll see some total stranger coming down the street, and I'll feel the urge to give the person one hell of a kick. I'll see someone coming on bike, and I'll get this urge to stick out my arm all of a sudden and clothesline the bastard, take the person down with one shot, stuff like that, you know, whatever."

Girl, you don't know what the hell you're saying.

"And yet you don't actually become violent, do you?"

"No."

"Then it's just fence-sitting, isn't it? I mean, in the sense that you're retreating from direct participation in the struggle?"

"Excuse me?"

For a moment I was so dumbfounded that I couldn't say a word. Give me a break. What the hell kind of vocabulary is that, huh? What decade do you think it is, you old bastard—is this the All-Campus Joint Struggle Committee or something? That country only exists in your imagination buddy you're living in Lilliput buddy I mean what the hell there's a pretty big difference between not hurting someone and "fence-sitting" as you call it what the fuck are you talking about old man what the hell am I supposed to do with you what the fuck you want me to fucking rip you to pieces huh? My thoughts were still racing along when—

"What does 'fence-sitting' mean?" asked the television girl.

And the whole room froze.

After that the old guy unveiled his screwed-up two-premises-and-a-backward-slide brand of syllogism, advancing the frightening proposition that since there was a gap between getting frustrated on the one hand and attacking people or pulling knives on the other, since there was this gap, and since there was no way you could explain the presence of this gap, he'd like to work on the assumption that there is no gap, and meanwhile the television girl kept giving us her two points over and over again, which were: Like, don't you think each of us must have one or two people that he or she wants to kill, you know? and: I mean, I kind of think it would just be like *so exciting*, you know, and I'm pretty sure that *everyone* in my generation feels that way, seriously . . . The conversation went on like that, with the two of them totally failing to connect with each other, which is actually kind of interesting in its own right, kind of like listening to a fun-and-easy course in basic philosophy or something, with terms like Eros and Thanatos and Oedipus complex and separation anxiety strewn about here and there, and I kept my mouth shut. My eyeballs kept repeating the same silent ping-pong motions; I felt the way I would have done if I'd been there to gather material for an article. Retreating into perfect silence, my thoughts became completely occupied by a desire for booze. Alcohol is, after all, the quickest way to relieve tension.

They say you shouldn't take psychotropic drugs when you're drinking, though, to tell the truth, I've done it myself lots of times. The reason is that alcohol acts as a very strong organic solvent. Alcohol will dissolve just about anything, forming an alcohol solution. The brain protects itself from injury by shutting out most of the substances it might come into contact with—it does this with something called the blood-brain barrier—but alcohol is able to get through with no problem. That's why drinking is one of the oldest of humanity's pleasures; that's the reason. So what happens when you take drugs with alcohol is that they work too well, and they hit you really fast—they aim straight for your brain. The brain is mostly lipids; it's basically fat. Since alcohol is an organic solvent and will dissolve just about anything organic, it can dissolve fat. I continued to keep my mouth shut, hoping only that the debate would hurry up and end.

It hit me when I saw myself reflected in the glass of the Family Mart fridge.

When I was drinking I always thought I was just drinking, that was all; alcoholism was a problem for old geezers in some other world. But in fact I was totally dependent. I was dependent, I wanted to use alcohol as the organic solvent it actually is, use it to dissolve the ever-present, unavoidable feeling that I was out of place, that what was outside my skin didn't match. And inside my skin—myself, so small, always shivering, always quivering. To let that self out, to let it stream into the outer world, without feeling out of place. To make it possible for me to chatter away on the phone, just as I want. To let myself burst into laughter over a silly story. To shorten the emotional distance I have to go before I can cry for someone.

It was . . . I don't know—I don't think I can say it very well. It was just that I'm on the side of people who don't want to kill, who don't want to harm other people. Which is the same as saying that I want to avoid breaking people and even things as much as possible, I want to hurt them as little as possible, and I feel this with a passion so strong I could cry. But the problem was all that went hand-in-hand with admitting my own weakness, my own incompetence, and I wanted to forget that, and so once again—I would drink.

The craving for alcohol returned.

I only throw up alcohol when it's inevitable, or when there's some practical reason for me to do so, because the smell and the acidity are too much for me. Which is to say that if you want to have fun while you vomit, you've got to vomit good food. It's totally perverted. I never wanted to be doing anything like this. The thought of life without vomiting

linked itself, in my mind, in no time at all, with a
desire for alcohol. I didn't even have the right to
laugh at that old bastard's screwed-up syllogism . . .
except that I could feel the truth of mine. Alcohol
entering my bloodstream directly through the
mucous membranes. No peristalsis. Alcohol,
absorbed in that way, circulating through my blood
vessels—that was the only thing that could help me
now.

A fast, wet snow had started falling over Tokyo.

One bottle of white wine, one bottle of gin. Anise
vodka was what I really felt like drinking but they'd
sold out. After putting the bottles in my basket I
headed over to the magazine rack by the door and
grabbed a few things that caught my eye. One of the
magazines was supposed to have something of mine
in it but I was afraid to look. My mind just wants
me to hurry up and give it some booze; there's a
second mind doing whatever it can to annoy the
first—these people in my head don't get along. The
one trying to piss off the one who's begging for
booze isn't concerned or anything, she's not trying
to hold her back, that's not it; she's just being
nasty. My thoughts and my actions are completely
disconnected. I start leafing through a few of the
magazines. Drinking and vomiting are both terrible,
painful problems, but they don't show up anywhere. Not a single one of these magazines even
mentions them; it's as if things like that only occur

on some distant planet. I feel more of a connection with magazines targeting teenage motorcycle gangs. I have more faith in girls hooked on speed. I feel more sympathy for these young women who confess that they still want to stay with their boyfriends, no matter what happens.

Is it just me? Am I the only one?

I got so irritated I couldn't stand it anymore. And I was afraid of the voices . . . I'm yearning to have just a single, strong current of thought. Standing here lost in my reading, poring over the pages of some magazine. Miura Risako. Who the hell is she? Oh yeah, yeah, that's right—Miura Kazu's wife. The soccer guy. What team was he on again, Verdy Kawasaki? Why the hell do you even know that, huh? When did you start either putting or letting J League trivia into your head? says one of the voices, and even though I tell it to stop that's unleashed them and now I've got all sorts of voices going off in my head, doing what they like, staging a "Can You Match the City with the J League Team Quiz"! Bellmare . . . Hiratsuka. Kashiwa? Reysol. Jubilo . . . Iwata . . . Kyoto? Purple Sanga . . . Urawa . . . Reds. Shut the fuck up. YOKOHAMA! Two separate voices go off in stereo, shouting at the same time, evidently competing, one saying Marino, the other saying Flugels, and then yet another voice cuts in with an OK, OK, well while we're at it, how 'bout GANBA and CEREZO in *OSAKAAAAAA!*—and I almost explode.

"Wow, so she's got a kid, has she?" I say quietly to myself, aloud. Once again I'm lost in my reading, poring over the magazine. I don't care if it's Miura Risako or someone else; I don't care who it is, I just want to get back over to my own side. "I bet there aren't many women besides me who'd keep riding their exercise bikes right into the ninth month," says Miura Risako. "And sure enough, she still looks just as great as she did when she was working as a model," the text continues. Then Miura Risako comes back in quotes: "I really felt a sense of urgency, you know? It was like, I have to get myself back—it's now or never."

A sense of urgency.

Have to get myself back—now or never. A sense of urgency.

If I don't do it now, I never will.

"Relaxation is the motif during weekends with my hubby. But you won't find any down-home casuals here—instead, elegant black casuals from Ralph Lauren and Emporio Armani set the tone, with caps and sneakers adding a little extra tang." Listen ass-hole, how the hell are you supposed to relax if you turn it into a fucking motif? Relaxation: the work you do on your days off. Great, that's just great. The fuckers. But who the hell am I angry at . . . ? Just then, for the first time in almost ten years in the business, I truly grasped what it means to edit. All magazines have to be edited. Of course, you've got editing in movies and soap operas and things like that, too. The question is: just what does it mean to edit? The editor endeavors to create an image of a certain person or group of people by accumulating scenes and episodes. To make each and every one of these scenes, she or he must select the moments that give off the most brilliant light and string them together, and then all the parts that have been cut, tons and tons of them, have to be scrapped. Parts trashed for the sake of selected parts, chucked out together with all the work that went into making them—all the monotony, the boredom, the exhaustion, the depression—unfavorable conditions, that's how things are day after day after day, and we live the greater part of our lives on the side of everything that gets cut.

Even when an article is talking about "The Simple Pleasures of a Leisurely Life" or something, it's been put together using only the bits that sparkle, nothing else. It's been edited; it's not real life. You think Miura Risako never spends her days off in a sweatsuit? You think she's *never* done that? That she never spends the whole day in her pajamas because it takes too much energy to get dressed? That she's never felt emotionally unstable? Oh sure, there are plenty of times when I just get so bored and lonely, yes, and my husband goes away for games all the time, sometimes I just feel completely out of sorts that maybe twenty or thirty times a day I start wanting to call him up on my mobile and talk. Do you think that's abnormal? Of course, when they're in the middle of practice or something, I know there's no way for him to get away, I'm perfectly aware of that, it's just that there's nothing to do, I'm so lonely, and the baby . . . Sometimes I kind of start to hate my husband, you know, and then I stop feeling any genuine affection for the baby, like I can't love him from the heart, you know, and then sometimes I just get this urge to slap him, I really do. That kind of thing doesn't ever show up in any of the parenting magazines. It makes me so afraid, maybe I'd better go and see a therapist, do you think that would be wise? murmurs one of the voices inside me, standing in for Miura Risako, except that the real Risako would never say these things; and even if she did, it would all be edited out. She's independent, she's natural! That's the woman. That's what these editors construct. And housewives perform their lives from these editorial scripts. Yeah, I remember that at a certain point you started coming across these odd-balls—I don't really want to call them Wives with Talent so how about Celebrity Wives; you know who I mean. Hori Chiemi might have been the first. It was probably around then, I'm not sure, and then you had women like Mita Hiroko and Miura (maiden name Shitara) Risako and so on, who married when it became clear they didn't have much longer in the entertainment industry, and then lived the life of status—they became the women housewives present and future yearned and would yearn to be. Who was that other one? There was another woman like that pretty recently, married that champion shogi player, Habu Yoshiharu, a woman you see even now on the packs of tissues money-lenders pass out on the street as advertisements. Yeah, I remember how surprised I was to see her, to see . . . To see who? is what I'm thinking now, and the answer is: Hatada Rie. Hold on. Maybe it was Ikuina Akiko on the tissues? Whatever, it probably matters quite a lot to the husband but it doesn't mean a bean to the media. Ultimately the gap between the Celebrity Wife's lifestyle, described in the magazines, and your own life is all that really matters, that's what motivates consumption—

Depression. It's what you discover in the interval between a perfect zero and a sense of accomplishment, that's everyday life, that's depression . . .

Depression is looking at the perfectly blank screen of your computer the moment before you start writing. To take just one example.

Perhaps the urge to escape that feeling is what induced me to start collecting other people's words. To have other people's stories match my own, to have my own words exist on the outside, the strange feeling of omnipotence you get when you seem connected to the world. Gathering words, linking them—linking them because when you do you start to see links that were invisible before. You have the sense that you're the one making the world go around. Everyone speaks in fragments, but for an instant those fragments are a catalyst, my self is erased and it brings on a wave of pure ecstasy, that instant is the drug, I'm seized by the drug, I yearn to relive that drugged moment in its perfect form— and so I would write, but every time when I finished I found that only a part of the world had been repro- duced, that was all, it didn't matter how many words I borrowed from other people's mouths, the work of gathering and arranging them was still mine and if I arranged them well I got the credit, but ultimately all the labor that involved would rob me of my youth and beauty. The thing is, it's hard to go on living without sometimes feeling a sense of achievement, and being beautiful and feeling like an achiever are two things that don't work well together. And yet, almost all the magazines suggest that you figure out a way to do both. Not enough material for a special issue, so they suggest doing it both ways. Try one, try the other, give it all a try, they suggest. Hey, what you're saying now sounds kind of different from what you were saying last week, doesn't it? If you really want to preserve your beauty, don't expect to enjoy too many accomplishments. Live life in moder- ation. Don't cross any lines, don't let yourself be attracted by anything on the far side of the line. This is probably the truth; the people sending and receiving are most likely Celebrity Wives and their supporters. If you believe what the magazines say, your income can never be large enough, you won't even have enough for food, you can cut your food expenditure down into negative numbers and still you'll never catch up, so you've got to start by marrying someone rich. All in order to consume. You'd think this was some sort of special concept, but now for the first time I realized that it was in fact the essence of every one of these magazines and the advertisements they carried. The truth is, they don't tell many lies.

I've been involved in just about every aspect of this business. The editing of women's magazines included. I've done it all, everything you have to do to give readers reasons to consume, creating desire in the gaps, in the intervals between depression and boredom and the monotony of work, between the selected and the rejected parts. Relaxation is the motif during weekends with her hubby, but she certainly never lets herself become *too* casual. The gap between this image and a certain someone somewhere who spends the whole day feeling awful in her pajamas, this gap gives you a reason to consume. So outside of work, in my own personal life, I ended up trapped in a cycle I had designed. I stopped being able to see where I started, where others ended. Saving only the most gorgeous scene, tossing all the rest . . . .The utterly obvious fact is that life on *this* side has died.

After Miura Risako came an article on cosmetics. The title read, "How Up Are You on Environmental Cosmetics?" An unhealthy environment may well be damaging your skin—if it is, we suggest you give environmental cosmetics a try. One of the best-known environmental beauty creams is all the rage in

Europe now: "La Prairie Defense Shield" combines
ten different kinds of antioxidants gently to protect
your skin from everything in your environment that
could cause it to age. In the past, environmental
cosmetics were seen as little more than tools to help
keep skin feeling fresh, and they had a reputation for
being slow to take effect; but now this new generation
of cosmetics has cleared those hurdles. The products
are lined up on the page, each one the same size.
Flip a few pages and there's an advertisement.

The copy:

"You must have noticed by now. Subtle changes
are already becoming visible in your skin . . . . Many
women suffer this kind of skin damage . . . . It's not
an inevitable decline—" My eyes stop. I swallow.

It's not an inevitable decline—

"It's not an inevitable decline, but a lack of balance
that's at the root."

A new concept to help you regain the balance
your skin has lost, nature's way!

"It's not an inevitable decline." If I had been the
copywriter, I would have underlined that; it's the
whole point of the ad.

It's not your fault. You're not in decline.

Let us give you a hand. We'll protect you from
your environment.

Listen, people, let me write these for you. I'll
show you how to take it one step further, I'll pinpoint
the place where you need to apply the pressure.
After all, I'm *made* of other people's feelings.

When I go out to get material for a story, the male reporters tend to say things. Your skin's been looking kind of bad lately, hasn't it? Seems like you've put on some weight, huh? Of course, if I've lost weight, I've lost weight, and they point out that, too: Hey, you're getting pretty skinny, aren't you? You've got bags under your eyes, seriously—not getting enough, huh? You getting laid lately, girl? OK, it's true that when a woman hasn't been eating or sleeping it does tend to show more than it would in a man, but why the hell should I have to be subjected to remarks like that just because I'm female? Men don't say that sort of thing to each other. It's none of your damn business, I'm my own person, I think, but even then in some other corner of my brain I'm thinking, I can stop this, but maybe if I don't act now, it'll be too late.

I have to go and buy this tomorrow. Make a mental note: number one on my list of priorities. Which is the nearest department store that carries this brand . . . . Same old thing. Come on, you know better than anyone around that nothing that dramatic is going to happen; hell, you've worked as a copywriter, you ought to know that better than anyone. A self-mocking laugh bubbled up inside me, creating a painful itch in my throat. Ha ha. So you think you're ugly. Yes, but that's not your fault, it isn't true that you've become ugly. It's just that you're under a lot of stress these days, I'm sure that's all it is, you'll get back to normal. You'll return to normal you'll return to normal you'll return to normal.

It starts looping.

Environmental stress environmental stress environmental stress environmental stress—

Stop it, just stop . . .

The weak voice is back—in no time at all it fills my body.

It's the same as always, you just get stuck in the same loop, that's all. You are who you are, isn't that enough? You won't feel any confidence in yourself until you win the applause of the masses, is that it?

Yeah, maybe. But even so.

I tried to walk to the register.

Hey, want an ice cream?

It was the same voice.

Ice cream? This voice hardly ever surfaces. And it doesn't surface alone when it's quiet. "Ice cream, ice cream," I murmured, and already, like a puppet on a string, I was heading in that direction. There was a man walking towards me from the corner of the ice cream freezer, way down at the end of the aisle.

Hickory-stripe overalls with the legs tucked down a bit into navy-blue and yellow boots. Rubber boots. It's only just started snowing, around midnight, and this is Tokyo. An odd way to dress. Looks like a fisherman. But I like the look. A broad chest and smooth, round shoulders. His chest. His hair. Perfectly straight, a bit long at the front. May have the tiniest bit of a curl, because it rises just a tad at the hairline and then spills down, parting naturally to the left and right. The soft line joining his neck to his chest. The swell of his chest muscles, hidden behind the top of his overalls. He's just a bit tall.

The creatures inside me start going crazy. Something puddled in my mouth. It took a while for me to realize that it was saliva. Lately my saliva always had a sour taste to it—I no longer remembered the taste it had back when it was pure. My pulse quickened.

The voices were going wild.

But like a column of air bubbles, more than you can count, streaming up from the sea floor towards the water's surface, they mixed and tangled, making it impossible to understand what any particular voice was saying. It was like hearing laughing and speech on the other side of a wall, listening to a crowd of people in the room next door, when all you know is that they're talking but you can't make out what they're talking about. Go on, say something, start chattering away like you always do, go on. Slowly swallowing my spit, I let my consciousness sink down a little and tried to tune in on one of the voices—any of them would be fine, I didn't care which—and then all at once the whole mass of them began writhing, within me, churning as if they were boiling. The voices erupted like an explosion; there was so much information that it was just like having no meaning at all. I felt like I was suffocating, I couldn't even manage to moan. For a moment a moist sensation blessed my dry skin, and I felt that the voices had plastered themselves all over the surface of my body.

I want to eat.

It was the voices, but it wasn't a sound. The message was communicated as a forceful mass of meaning directly into every corner of every cell in my body.

I want to eat. I want to eat that.

I want to eat.

But this was me, no one but me, my own intention, the voice became something that wasn't a voice but my own self, plastered over the surface of my body— I was teasing the man forward with my eyes. The voices disappeared, the interior of my body fell silent and now it was utterly empty, there was something cowardly trembling in the emptiness, something that knew no language.

Centered now on the surface of my skin, I sought the man's eyes with my own. I squinted just a little, channeling all the energy in my body into my eyes. And then, within a space as wide as my narrowed eyes, the density of the air changed, the pressure climbed, and a woven-together line like string stretched through space to the man. He accepted it. He lifted his chin just a shade, signaling that he had taken it, then squinted a little, just as I had. A string of high-pressure air shot back at me from his side and suddenly the two of us were tied together, and then—precisely at that moment—I was seized by a violent shaking.

I had no idea what had happened. I couldn't even speak; the only sound I could get out of my throat was the gasp of air being inhaled. My pulse quickened. The first thing that occurred to me was that it was an earthquake, so I covered my head and glanced around. Inside and outside of me everything was rocking violently, but no one was panicking. The interior of the store, still bathed in light. People reading magazines. The man is staring right at me, totally unfazed.

It was the mobile in my breast pocket, vibrating.

Even after I figured this out, it took a while for reality to return. I'm wondering how the man could possibly be controlling my phone—what's going on here?

This can't be happening.

What the hell? What the hell? *What the hell?*

I'm slightly bent over. The man's staring at the part of me that's vibrating.

This just isn't possible.

Oh my god, it's brain death, it must be brain death, that's the only reason I'd get a call at this time of night! My journalist self had returned. I had been thinking about writing an article on brain death and organ transplants, so I'd asked a hospital to contact me whenever a relevant patient came in, no matter what time it was. There's a technique now that makes it possible to delay brain death—one that always works. It's called hypothermic therapy. If you lower the person's body temperature, you can extend the time it takes for the brain to stop functioning; the only thing is that if you keep it at that low temperature

too long then the other organs necrotize. You need
lots of skill and lots of experience to be able to
identify the precise moment when the necessary
balance has been attained. This isn't particularly
new information. What interested me was that this
one hospital, which was famous for hypothermic
therapy, was now leading the field in organ transplants as well. In other words, on the one hand, you
had doctors struggling to draw out a patient's life to
the very limit, while on the other hand, you had
people whose only hope lay in waiting for some
other patient to die. I wanted to do a careful,
detailed exploration of the drama inherent in the
conflict between these two very different stand-
points. Was one of the patients I'd met previously in
a critical condition? Or had a new patient just been
brought in to Casualty?

I've gotta answer. I've gotta go. I've gotta answer.
I've gotta go. I keep repeating the words like a spell,
but I'm paralyzed; my body refuses to move. Brain
death. Is this how it feels? Your body is alive and still
warm, all the fluids are flowing, but the commands
aren't reaching their destinations, extremities
growing cold, your body temperature can't be controlled, shaking, twitches, peristalsis, eyeballs moving,
breathing at the slowest possible rate, only the involuntary muscles move, you can't coordinate your own
movements.

The man kept drawing closer but I couldn't take
a single step. The phone had vibrated seven times

since I'd started counting . . . then, as soon as the man drew up beside me, it stopped. The fluids in my body were still sloshing around but my thoughts gradually gravitated towards flatness. Way down in the deepest depths of my churning body fluids there is a region untouched by the movement. What is this place? This body here is all there is, this is me. I'm five feet three—maybe three and a half—inches tall, no more, yet this place feels like it's dozens and dozens of miles down. The man walked past me, brushing the back of my hand with his palm. It was damp. Warm. And I was cold. I could feel everything, right down to the roughness of the skin in the lines of his hand. I heard the sound of our two jackets, each made of a different material, brushing against each other. Nothing in me could move. By the time he passed a step beyond me, I had already forgotten what the sound was like. I was dying to turn around but I couldn't move; couldn't make myself move. The smell of his hair hung in the air. What kind of shampoo is that? I like the smell. The sound of the damp rubber soles of his boots striking the linoleum floor, slipping slightly: the unique sound of departing steps.

You've got to get up and go, wo wo wo—

Suddenly I'm able to hear a song, a fun sort of melody. My senses are back to normal! This is the store's song, and I can hear it! Gotta get up and go. OK, but where? There's only one thing in my head: I want to eat that. Wait a second, wait, this isn't right at all, that's the Lawson's song and this is Family Mart, you're still hallucinating, says a little boy's voice. Whatever, kid, I don't give a shit, I want to go, I want to live, I want to go on living, I'm living.

Most of the time actions like standing and walking and stuff were things I'd taken care of unconsciously. Now, when I attempted to make my feet move, my fingers might start twitching or something—the commands and the actions were getting muddled. When your whole body is in a state of tension, waiting for a signal, there's no telling what might link with what. I improvised a method for getting myself to move. First of all, I had to keep the rules as simple as possible. I imagined several nerve endings, then summoned an image of them transmitting a nerve impulse and stopping, then transmitting another and stopping again, as if the whole process were as simple as Morse code, just a series of ons and offs. I gave the cells just one extremely simple rule to follow—all they had to do was behave in the same fashion as the next cell in the line. If I could just manage to convey the vector to the first cell, everything down to the extremities would move in the appropriate direction. The important thing was to have a cell that functioned really well in the first position. That's how flocks of birds manage to stay in formation, and what makes it possible for them to execute such crisp, beautiful changes in direction. I seem to remember hearing that's how ants move, too. I didn't care how primitive the method was, I just wanted to move.

I moved. I changed direction. I set the basket with the bottles in it down by my feet. I heard the clink of glass bumping glass. The clerk's eyes.

Walking like some kind of robot, I aimed for the exit. Only the door was bright; everything else had dissolved into darkness. The automatic door slid open. Two in the morning, Tokyo under a March snow. There was an umbrella if I needed one. It wasn't mine, but so what? There were lots, one two three four five si . . .

Who needs an umbrella?

As I look up, snow turns the world into a spindle. White flakes pour down on my face, melting quickly on my skin, seeping through my dry epidermis and down into the deeper layers. More and more of me is eaten away by this snow. Water used to bounce right off my skin, but take a look at me now. When I say "used to" I'm not talking about my teens or something—it was still like that about a year ago. If you live in a world that's controlled overwhelmingly by men, and if you don't want people making remarks about things that are really none of their business, you've either got to be totally indifferent to how you look or else go around looking beautiful all the time. I attempted to be beautiful all the time. But there are limits to how much you can do. The amount of time and work it'll take for me to stay beautiful certainly won't decrease. From now on it'll only take more effort, and of course all that is added to the other things I have to do as a working member of society. And I'm bound to age, little by little, there's no escaping that . . . Just the thought of fighting it makes me so irritated and depressed I can't stand it. And what if I can't manage to give up the vomiting and the booze? Maybe I started doing all these things because I was tired of being beautiful. Or maybe it was because I wanted to forget the depression.

You've gotta get up and go.

The song by Moritaka Chisato keeps repeating endlessly in my head, just the one phrase, clashing in a peculiarly relaxed way with my jittery mood. I have no idea whether I'm actually pumping air through my vocal chords, singing along, or whether it's just someone performing in my head. You've gotta get up and go. It hasn't been that long, he can't have gone very far. If I run after him, I should be able to catch up. All these voices except the one singing Moritaka's song have gone silent. But was that voice real or was it just a memory or what? There was that time I spent the whole day drinking the gin she advertises, yeah, I started in the morning, I remember that, Gin gin gin, you're French if you mix it with something or other—what was it again?— I remember I started drinking to get rid of a hangover, that was how it started, I looked in my mirror and my face was so puffy I couldn't bear it . . . All these memories coming back; take a look at the instant replay.

My field of vision is extremely narrow. And low. The snow keeps sinking into me more and more, soaking me. My strides aren't even a quarter their normal length. I keep trying to step with my right foot while I'm using it as the axis of motion, doing stuff like that, and I almost fall. Different parts of my body are having trouble cooperating; each part tries to move on its own, so that most of the time I can't even walk straight. My gaze refuses to settle. Is my head wobbling? I don't have time to waste trying to figure out why everything is so scattered, use your brain, girl, you've gotta go. Only my will to move keeps me moving. I will myself to follow the man; maybe I don't have enough will power to waste on anything else, which is why I have so little control over my body. Something, perhaps my spirit, is running on ahead of me, all by itself, out of sync with my body. My eyes zoom around randomly, totally unconnected to my consciousness, snipping out still shots and pasting them directly to my retina. I see a car coming towards me about a hundred yards away and then all of a sudden it's right in front of me. I've already put my foot out into the pedestrian crossing, so now I'm being honked at. There's a gust of wind. A chaos of noise, a chaos of sensations.

I heard a sharp sound in the distance, cutting through the chaos.

My entire body moved as one. Inside me, countless cells lifted my head and started moving all at once in the same direction.

A whistle?

The sound came again.

Stretching my hand out in the direction of the sound, I lost my balance and fell to my knees in the snow. I wiggled forward a little, then worked my way through the sequence of motions necessary to stand up again. It was like trying to reassemble myself. The green WALK signal was flashing. Over there, at the end of the crossing, there was a housing development into which no cars were admitted: the sound came from a street that ran alongside the development. The signal had now turned red, but fortunately no cars were coming. Once I crossed, the whistle sounded closer. Gusts of March snow obscured my view. My eyes hurt, but I couldn't get them to blink properly. I couldn't see anyone. I moved forward, relying solely on the sound to guide me. Where are you? It's you, isn't it? Man, if you're going to whistle, you might as well come and get me. Yeah, OK, I know, I've gotta go, I'm the one who's gotta go. I'm the one who felt the hunger, after all.

There was no one in the place where the whistles ended. Something large was blocking my way. I looked up. The thing was navy blue, enormous, smooth. My vision was still blurry and my sensations came only in fragments, so at first I couldn't tell what it was.

Arms spread, moving my hands across its surface, I stood up.

It was a truck.

"Oh!"

I let out a cry. The man I'd seen earlier was in the driver's seat. Who'd have guessed the guy was a trucker? I was only looking for a person, which is why I had so much trouble finding him. He grinned down at me, narrowing his eyes a bit as if he were staring into a glare, the way he had when we'd first run into each other. I found myself on the verge of tears. Tears actually fell from my eyes, but they disappeared almost immediately into the snow. A bag of ice from Family Mart is hanging from the windshield wipers. He must leave it there because it's so cold outside. He pointed to the door on the other side. I lifted the silver handle and the door popped open. Warm air streamed out. The step was extremely high. I placed my foot on top of it.

"Grab on up there," he said.

There was a grip on the ceiling for you to hold. I hoisted myself into the seat, dragging myself up. A white world lay spread before me, below me. The area I knew so well seemed to have changed into a vast plain. Maybe it had something to do with the windshield, which was larger and more curved than that of a regular car—everything in my field of vision seemed to have widened. There was a small window set into the door, down by my feet, and that made it seem as if I were hovering mid-air, made me feel as if I were rising up into the snow rather than sitting with the snow streaming down on me.

"Welcome."

Being here is like being in this man's womb, I thought. There were no decorations, but it was comfortable, it was soft and warm. The man gave me a towel. The sudden change in temperature made me start shivering.

This room is his body and my heart. He's up high and I'm pierced by his gaze. I'm being watched as I chase after him, crumbling, tumbling down to the ground and crawling all the way here. He's got the upper hand right from the start.

"You were watching me all along, from up here?"

"No, not all along. I mean, I didn't really think you'd come."

I felt grateful for the snow—since my skin was wet, he wouldn't notice how bad it was.

Just looking at his skin, I could see that it was dreadfully smooth. The voices started acting up for a moment, then fell silent. I no longer knew what to say.

"You want a drink? It's shoochuu, pretty strong stuff."

"Sure."

The trucker went outside and got the bag of ice that was hanging from the windshield wipers. When he transferred the ice to the plastic cups, flakes of snow that were stuck to the bag adhered to the surface of the cubes. He poured the shoochuu, then added some bitter lemon. The snap ice makes as it melts. I gazed through the rough crust of snow on

one of my ice cubes. The bitter lemon was hardly
sour at all, there was only a faint trace of that special
citrus sharpness, and the drink had no odor—it
reminded me of the soda I drink to help me throw
up. Except that this cocktail the man had made for
me tasted good. I wanted the voices back. Come on
guys, all of you, start going wild again, tell me you
want this man. I can't do it on my own. I can't do it
sober. They say there's no hangover when you're
drinking shoochuu, but for some reason I wasn't
even getting drunk. I'll have to get drunk, at the very
least. Man, I've come this far already. I can't do it
sober. This was the first time I'd ever come on to a
guy I didn't know, someone I'd never seen before.
There was an open bag of some kind of puffed-corn,
junk food, so I asked the man if I could have some,
then ate a few. It's good, I thought. "This is good,
isn't it?" I said quietly. I had no idea whether I was
talking to the man or to someone inside me, hoping
to provoke a response.

"How old are you?" he asked.

"Thirty-one." I told him my real age without
hesitation. For some reason I just didn't feel like
trying any of those tricks on him.

"No kidding? You're older than me, then."

"Yeah, I figured I was. How old are you?"

"Twenty-six."

"Huh. I would've thought you were younger . . ."

"I saw you had a bottle of wine and a bottle of
gin."

"Yeah . . . I've got people coming over this weekend." I had no bags or anything so I had to think quick. "But I decided to forget it. I started thinking, you know—I mean, after all, it's only Wednesday."

"It's Thursday, actually."

There was a moment of silence.

"You wanna watch TV?"

"Sure."

There was a tuner on top of the dashboard and on top of the tuner there was a small television. We watched a comedy for a while, then changed the channel. They were broadcasting the opening ceremony of the Paralympics.

"Man," said the man, "they're awesome."

People standing up and people in wheelchairs were dancing in pairs on the small screen. Those in the wheelchairs kept spinning around in time with the music, doing it so elegantly it surpassed description. In the center there was a column of fire. It seemed to be kind of different from the Olympic torch, but the screen was so small that I couldn't really make it out.

"God, these guys are awesome!"

Watch the fire, dance, drink. I felt as if I'd grasped what it meant to be happy in ancient times. The singer on the screen sang what appeared to be the Paralympic theme song. It was a hundred times better than the Olympic theme song, and the ceremony as a whole was more than a thousand times

better than the opening ceremony for the Olympics.
I mean, what the hell, Ozawa Seji is famous the
world over, blah blah blah, whatever you say, why do
you want to go and play Beethoven's *Ninth* when
you're holding the Olympics in Japan, huh, why the
hell do you have to sing a piece from Germany? The
music you hear in the background at all the big
moments is from *Madame Butterfly*—I mean, hello,
musical director Asari Keita, are you completely
stupid or just brainless? The huge fan breaks and
Itoo Midori steps out in make-up that makes her
look like Raggedy Ann or something—man, that
gave me a shock, let me tell you, the words "national
disgrace" must have been thought up especially for
that day. And Hagimoto Kin'ichi's speech during
the ceremony—it was like a ventriloquist's act or
something, seriously, and why the hell are you
dragging out an old fuddy-duddy like Hagimoto
anyway, what's up with that? When my mind
rekindles an old fury I shift into drive and start
motormouthing. The me that's angry is an adult,
and yet for some reason the words that emerge
from my mouth are those of a child. When I start
cursing my mind shifts into gear. but right now it's
like the clutch is slipping, the engine is spinning
but the energy isn't being communicated to the
outside, that's the feeling—a weird sensation. But
not one I dislike.

The wheelchairs keep spinning smoothly right to
the end.

"Pretty cool song, isn't it?" he said.

"Yeah, it is. You know, when I first saw you . . ."

There was a knock on the driver's-side door. bonk bonk.

The man opened the window. It was a policeman. My body tensed briefly.

"Hey there. I got a report about someone idling in a residential area, but with it as cold out as it is tonight I can hardly tell you to cut the engine can I . . . ?"

"Hard to be a cop in this weather, too, I bet."

The man held out his license. In all the years I'd been alive, I'd never had any idea that truckers and policemen were on such friendly terms.

"Mr. . . . Okabe. How do you pronounce your first name?"

"Takatoshi. Hey, tell me, is there a park or something close by? I can't make my delivery until morning."

"Huh. It's the 'ki' for 'hope,' but you say it 'taka.' Kind of unusual, isn't it?"

"I don't know. I suppose so."

When the exchange with the police officer ended, we decided to park in front of the cemetery at the back of the train station. The man kept turning the steering wheel slightly one way or the other, muttering things about the dumbass who'd told us to take a street like this one, which was narrow and lined with stores, but we managed to squeeze through to the other side. Long banners had been hung out along the street; one of them fluttered against the glass. I shrank back instinctively.

"You seem to be on pretty good terms with the police."

He parked in the big circle in front of the cemetery, leaving the engine running.

"It's 'cause I'm out working, too, probably."

Yeah, that makes sense.

"How long have you had the truck?"

"Abut seven years, I suppose."

"And before that?"

"I used to work for a building contractor, then I bought the truck and started out as an independent. Had another rig before I got this baby."

"What's an independent?"

"It means I'm free."

"Why trucking?"

"Well, I don't have much education. Hardly even went to high school."

"I didn't realize you could just skip out on compulsory education."

"I don't know. I suppose maybe they give you something when you finish junior high, don't they, some sort of certificate or something? I didn't go to graduation either, though, so I don't know if I got one or not."

My next question was pretty dumb: "Why didn't you go?"

"No particular reason. I just didn't like it." He laughed.

This guy is healthy, I thought. I felt it instinctually. It had been a completely natural thing for him—he just refused to stay in a place he didn't like.

I let the seat support my body and buried my cheek in the short, fuzzy material that covered it. This is his body. I felt the vibrations of the idling engine in my chest and my skin, and it was as if he had enveloped me. Suddenly I understood why the voices were silent—it was because they felt safe. The vibrations had broken them down into the elements out of which they were originally composed; they no longer existed in the form of language. All the voices had dissolved into one another; they were circulating through my body like some composite solution. In the midst of the vibrations, I could make out my heartbeat.

"You were saying something about when you first saw me, right?"

"Oh yeah," I laughed. I remembered the words I had been about to say when the policeman arrived and they were cut off. "I think I was going to say that the boots were what drew me."

"Yeah, it's not really because of this snow, though. I mean, it just happens to be snowing in Tokyo, too. It snows all the time in Niigata."

"Why Niigata?"

"There are a lot of furniture factories there. Shizuoka, too, but most of them are in Niigata. See that apartment building they're putting up over there? I've got to deliver a load of doors there."

There was a brief silence, during which it started growing noisy again inside me. The voices are only able to relax as long as the words keep coming.

"So you keep the engine running all night?"

Reduce CO_2 Emissions, Stop Global Warming, Protect the Ozone Layer . . . Stuff like that flits through my mind, but it doesn't come as words—it's as if the concepts have been compressed, something like that.

His answer comes immediately. "Yup."

"Why don't you bring in a portable stove or something?"

"I'd run out of oxygen with a fire, right?"

"What about an electric heater or an electric blanket?"

"I'd need a generator for that."

Yeah, I suppose so. This truck is a generator. It's working as a generator this very moment. I start to feel that since we've got it on to keep us warm tonight, it doesn't matter if the world ends up dying tomorrow. The words have stopped. Just then the engine grew louder, and for a second the needle on the tachometer swung way over.

"Hey . . ." I'm going to tell him the truth, "I want to touch you."

"Um . . . you can if you want to."

He proffered his cheek as if to say that I could punch him, if that was what I wanted. He gave me a very mild, well-mannered smile. He had a way of narrowing his eyes ever so slightly that seemed to be a characteristic of his, and when he did his face took on a friendly, slightly dazzled look. The bridge of his nose was well formed, the tip came to a point. The area just around his mouth had a sort of sweet look to it, and he only had to move his lips a few millimeters to create a smile. His slightly long hair swayed.

"I'm afraid."

I listened to myself speaking as if the words were coming from some unknown place. I'd had no idea I would say that. Concentrating on the feeling, I realized there was a part of me that was wavering, quivering like jelly, like a jellyfish, and it was the same place that had spoken earlier, in that feeble voice, asking the others *please, please stop.* Basically this was a non-linguistic entity, and the linguistic bypass it took only appeared when I was extremely tense or when everything had become totally relaxed—the entity only detoured into language at times like that, seemingly by accident. Now the voices had submitted to the vibrations and the trembling entity had come directly into contact with the outside world. Or maybe my own trembling had fallen in line with the trembling of the idling engine.

"I'm sorry, I shouldn't have said that. I don't know, I seem to feel that since I hardly know you, you might suddenly change and get violent with me—I just have trouble believing that people aren't like that. I wonder why. I mean, no one has ever hit me or anything. It's weird, isn't it? I'm really sorry I'm saying this."

The man remained silent—I couldn't tell if he'd heard what I was saying or not. Then, still without speaking, he moved back into the space between the seat and the trailer. The space was intended for sleeping: he had a futon and a pillow and some stuff laid out back there. He lay down, leaning his head against the window on the other side, preserving a distance between us that seemed natural. "I'm listening," he said, smiling. I felt a sense of relief—a sensation, not something I understood intellectually—and I cried as if something inside me had melted into tears and started leaking out.

"I want to touch you. I just want to touch you."

I caressed my seat as I wept. There was a moment of silence. My tears dripped down on to the fluff of the seat and hung there like tiny particles of mist. When I looked up again, the man spoke.

"You wanna come over here?"

I nodded, then climbed over the gear lever. My tears didn't stop. I got on top of him and he raised his upper body and we kissed. He closed the curtains over the windows and the one that separated the seats from the space in the back.

I'd been wanting to do this all along. Ever since I'd first seen him. Drawing in the saliva with our tongues, we tasted each other. Tears spilled down on to my lips. I tasted my own salty flavor. He licked the tears from my cheek and then covered my eyes with his lips, sucking them into a vacuum, sucking away my tears as they emerged. I kept my eyes open the whole

time—half my world was lost in blackness. The inside
of his mouth was a little warmer than my eyes, a little
warmer than my tears. He started with my right eye,
then performed the same series of actions on the left.
The tears kept spilling out, one after the other. He
slipped his tongue into my eye, licked around the border between eyeball and eyelid, making a complete
circle. It's hard to say whether my eyeballs were more
or less sensitive than I thought—they could feel the
slight roughness of his taste buds, but at the same
time they didn't flinch or anything, they just let him
do what he was doing. I felt the softness and
resilience of my own eyeballs. There was a numbness
there; one of my contacts slid across the surface of my
eye. My vision clouded. But I didn't want him to stop.
He ran his hand across my head. As if I were a little
kid. I kept kissing his neck while I worked at unbut-
toning his overalls. There were two hooks that you had
to pull down before you could slide off the buttons. I
removed the first layer of clothing from his upper
body, then removed the second, and then kissed his
naked chest. The clothes covering my lower half were
stripped away, and now I was under him.

"Is it OK if I lick you?" he asked.

"Huh?"

Before I could even reply, he had begun licking
my genitals. He lifted my legs into the air, opening
them out so they formed a V and resting them on his
naked shoulders. They perched there like two birds.

"This is great. It's so beautiful."

It was winter—my legs were rough and dry, and I hadn't put any polish on my toenails. He stuck his fingers in the moist place and opened it. The place hadn't neglected to moisten itself. His tongue crept over the areas that secrete the fluids, covering a wide territory. His tongue slipped up inside me. A small ray from an outside light leaked through the curtain behind me and illuminated my moistened part.

"Okabe Takatoshi . . . don't you want to know my name?"

"Your first name is enough."

What a sad thing to say.

"Rei. Hayakawa Rei."

"It's great. So beautiful."

"So beautiful it's great."

"It's great."

"Say my name."

"Rei, it's great. It's great. It's g-Rei-t."

I feel—

I feel like—

I've become something extremely good.

Combining trembles that rarely emerge as speech, I asked him why.

"It's just like two lips."

I wasn't sure who was saying this. The various molecules that comprised my body rubbed up against one another, generating heat. I could feel the trembling of the truck all the way down my back. His tongue squirmed through the folds of my slit like a warm mussel. My toes twitched reflexively.

"What do women do when they masturbate? Show me?"

I always do it through my underwear. I never touch myself directly. But even though I told him this he kept pleading with me to show him. I began running my middle finger along the underside of my clitoris. It grew, becoming clearly triangular in shape. It rose, emerged from the folds of skin around it. It occurred to me that I was never able to touch it like this, because it was never exposed.

"You don't do stuff with your breasts?"

"Get me wet."

I stuck out my fingers, slipped them into his mouth, moistened them thoroughly with his saliva. I started fondling my nipples with my wet fingers.

I love you, I love you, I love you, I love you, I love you, I love you, I love you, I love you—

But I can't say the words.

The big toe of my left foot slipped on the window behind the curtain, drawing a line across the foggy glass. My toe ended up on the knob of the gear lever. The vibrations shuddered up through my legs, making my whole body shake. All I could do was clench my fists. I sucked my thumb, grabbed the hair on his forehead; I felt the voices being released from a core I could only sense within me when I closed my eyes, there in the emptiness of my body; and then the material that the voices were made of came floating up to the surface, just like when you use detergent to take out a spot of grease, long columns of some substance moving in and enveloping the grease, sucking it out; it has something to do with the attraction between plus and minus ions, I forget how it works, but that's how it was when the voices arose. They took something from me and left with it, they pushed something out of me. The power I had felt earlier, when my whole body was seized with the urge to eat the man—that power gathered now on the surface of my skin, turning into something like a layer of oil.

I felt myself being replaced. Only this was nothing like the terrifying change that occurs in people with multiple personalities, which I had read about in books. It was like . . . it was like reaching the vapor-ization point or the melting point or the boiling point or whatever, there are certain temperatures at which any substance will change its state, it's a hundred degrees for water and for oil it's some other temperature, I don't know exactly how hot it is, it's different for everything, and by using those tem-peratures you're able to get the particular pure substances you need out of solutions containing all kinds of other things—what's that called again, that technique? All along, I was . . . I mean, all the "I"s in me . . . we were like a compound solution. Maybe it only hurt so much because my body was in a solid state. I always wore pretty clothes when I was out in the world, I always tried to keep up appearances, and yet at the same time the thing I really wanted, the one thing I truly desired, was my liquefaction.

"You have a condom?"

"Yeah."

"I want to do it with you."

I got on top and let my body sink. His penis disappeared from view, and our two crotches joined, his and mine, perfectly matched. The man was sweating from the heat from the blower. It was winter but he was sweating. Skin so beautiful you couldn't tell where the sweat was coming from. Skin so smooth it was scary, skin that became equally wet all over. My hand slipped whenever I touched him. And there was no hair on his body. Where the hell are his pores? I wrapped my legs desperately around his thighs. My hands just went on rubbing his back, up and down and up again. My hands slipped so easily over the hills of his back that his upper body seemed to be moving at an unbelievably slow speed. The spasmodic jerking of our hips was detached from all the rest—those movements had lives of their own. It didn't matter what I did, I could never love him enough. So I bit his ear. And as if that had been some sort of signal, the man slowly turned his body so that his upper half covered mine. My palms slid around so much on his chest that I had a hard time supporting his weight. Then suddenly my hands slipped completely out from under him, and I moaned quietly. He lifted himself, for a moment my body felt entirely weightless, and then as I slowly began to drop I felt my back being caught, ever so gently, as my head started to bend back in response he grabbed my hair and I shivered as my head halted in mid-fall. I gazed up without blinking at the face now approaching my own—a man I didn't know at all. There was a brief moment before my own lips were covered by his. I was being watched. I kept staring back at him for a long time, unable to blink. Once his lips had covered mine, he moved quickly. His tongue entered my mouth. Then, slowly, he sank back onto the sheet. I like this guy.

The man's chin. Adorable. That's where the groans come from when he moves, when I move. I watched a bead of sweat fall from his chin and trickle in a line down his neck. His skin was damp everywhere, so the line of sweat was extremely shallow, hardly there at all. His chest rose in a gentle swell, which his body then squeezed down towards his waist. I couldn't distinguish the borders between the individual muscles, but I could feel their elasticity, and I could see that this was a body that worked.

I lifted my hips and rubbed them against his. "Hold on, I'm gonna come if you start doing stuff like that," said the man, and I said, "That's OK," and then a series of tremors quivered through his stomach. A single drop of sweat dropped from his arching chin. Suddenly my mouth was wide open. A lukewarm salty tang spread over the mucous membranes in my mouth, heading simultaneously both down into my throat and up into my nostrils. This was the first time I'd ever felt an urge like that: to catch the sweat of a man on top of me in my mouth.

It had a flavor like table salt, but I sensed a faint hint of something different—something absent from the sweat that collects on the surface of the body, something that had just been pumped from deep within.

The man squeezed his chest against mine, pressed his face against my shoulder. He had started breathing in time with the tremors. His shoulders were heaving up and down, tracing large arcs, and his face and hair and shoulders were all so wet I had the impression the man was sobbing. The moment when a man ejaculates is just about as masculine as you can get, and yet I found that it was the exposed, defenseless nature of that moment that attracted me. I caressed his head, smoothed the hair below his ears back against his skin. It had a slight wave to it, too, and although earlier it had been light and dry, it was now twisted around the nape of his neck, forming a shape like a C. His body heaved up two or three times more, then collapsed, its energy spent. I wanted to savor his weight forever.

My body absorbs water. I know from the sound it's making that the snow has turned into rain. I'm surrounded by water. My skin is covered, but skin breathes most deeply when it's covered like this. In water, individual cells can absorb oxygen directly. I absorb the man's sweat as though it were a nutrient. Someone once told me that people only absorb things when they're in the form of a solution. That even the oxygen we use is first dissolved into water within us.

The snow melted without leaving so much as a skin of white on the ground. "It'll be light soon, that's how it is at this time of year." That's what the man said, and he was right. The morning sky flared up for a moment, and after that the air filled with white light. The man didn't waste a second putting on his clothes, and even though I knew that he didn't mean to be cold—this was a healthy sign of practicality in a man used to working with others—I still felt sad.

He drove the truck up to the building site. The wet tarmac gleamed, a surface of light stretching off into the distance. It took a little less than an hour for him to unload the doors. I made up my mind not to get dressed and waited for him there, naked, wrapped up in the bedding. The blanket contained the heat from my body, the futon hugged my skin. There was an odor of sweat, different from the one I'd smelled earlier. Once again I dozed.

I awoke to the sound of a door opening. The scenery had changed. The man unbuttoned the front of his overalls. Maybe the work had made him warm? Or maybe he had just gone to the bathroom?

He turned his back to me, then glanced over his shoulder. "Could you get the back for me?" He wanted me to raise his dangling braces, but I ignored his request. Still wrapped in the blanket, I darted up front and shut the curtain over the driver's-side windshield.

"Now you have to show me yours."

I'll look at you the way you looked at me.

"Not now. It's small, I don't want to."

"That doesn't matter."

"I want you to see me when I'm big."

"Why?"

"What do you mean, why? That's just how it is."

"Whether your prick is hard or not, you're still you, right?"

I closed the curtain over the passenger's-side windshield. This truck had a total of five curtains. Two that covered the windshield, one for each of the windows in the back, and one that separated the space in the back from the seats.

"Let me do you the way you did me."

I bent down over his crotch, concealing myself beneath the level of the window. His penis swelled in my mouth until it touched the back of my throat. Neither the curtain that shut off the space in the back nor the curtains over the back windows were drawn. He dragged his hands through my hair, tangling it. Of course, the only vehicles that would let you see into a truck as high off the ground as this one were other trucks or four-wheel drives with extremely high suspensions, and it was pretty unlikely that either of those types of vehicles would be coming around here this early; but even if they did, the seats blocked the view well enough that they wouldn't be able to see either of us. When I glanced behind the seat and out through the small window over the narrow space in the back, I could see the sun slowly climbing higher. With every minute, every second that passes, the earth turns. The bald tires of this truck—Okabe had told me that truckers leave on the same tires all winter—rumble across the face of the earth, and the earth goes on forever, and everything moves with the truck's vibrations. I sensed something very far away. The sounds of things very, very far away from this place. Each one of these sounds, every single one was different. A bird was twittering. I could hear the voices of children on their way to school. I raised my eyes.

The moment our eyes locked there was an energetic peal of laughter, it seemed to pierce me to the core, but I was sucking him so it couldn't be coming from me. Laughter tumbled down, hitting me like last night's snow.

Love me.

The laughter tumbled down, hit me. And my body, my true self, had no words, it had nothing but a certain kind of vibration, all you had to do was make it move, move it just a little, and it would try to find some place to adhere to. It was nothing like thought or meaning. No, it was like desire or hunger, and if you translated it, the words you'd get would be: love me, love me, love me, love me. Voices mingled in the container of trembling I had become, the voices within me whirlpooled and rose and settled and churned, drifting one way and then another through a light sleep that knew no meaning. My body temperature changed in a number of different ways, different parts were completely different temperatures—but in a number of ways, at different temperatures, they all boiled.

Di still at ion?

Words were sown like seeds within me, repeating, confirming what the distant, barely audible voice had said.

Distillation.

Using heat to extract certain components from a solution. Now I remembered. Distillation.

This time I had no idea whether I'd spoken the words aloud or not. Just then I sensed that every-thing was becoming still, sedated. My field of vision dissolved, and I fell.

I dozed.

The next thing I knew the seat was extended and I was naked in my blanket, and the man was clothed, nothing but his genitals exposed, and I was lying on top of him. I sat up again, but the man lay there for a while without getting up. I pulled up the front of his overalls. When had he put on this new condom? After climbing over the gear lever to the passenger's side, I reached back into the area behind the seat and gathered my clothes, then dressed. My body still remembered the laughter that had gusted through me, flurried down on top of me. But the willful, headstrong person I'd been just a short while ago was gone, she had dropped away like a layer of skin, and there was no way for me to retrieve her.

The man sat up. Do I remember his name? Okabe . . . *It's the "ki" for "hope" but you say it 'taka.' Kind of unusual, isn't it?* The character for "hope" floats up in my mind, filling one of the blanks in the puzzle. *How do you pronounce your first name . . . Takatoshi.*

The day after a snowfall is always bright. Signs showing the names of the towns we were passing through fell away behind us with perfect regularity; they hung under the traffic lights in every new town, but I couldn't link them together, I couldn't tell in which direction we were going. At the moment I had no idea where Okabe was going, when he needed to be there, what particular aspect of his work he would be doing. I didn't even know whether it was OK for me to be here with him or not. I had no idea what to do with myself. The snow I'd seen falling and melting in the morning light still lingered here. It couldn't be the latitude and it wasn't the altitude, so I kept wondering what kept it from melting, and then finally I hit upon the utterly obvious answer, that it was because the city generates much more heat than the little towns out here.

"Are we going to Niigata?" I asked, just to have somewhere to start.

"No, Kawaguchi."

"*Kawaguchi?*" The unexpected reply left me puzzled.

"I'm gonna get a load of tires. No point in driving with an empty truck."

"No, I guess not. Having it empty isn't good, is it?"

A train station appeared: the sign said "Misato." We went around a roundabout, passing a small noodle stand; a pachinko parlor; a ramen place; and a Mister Donut. Then once more the flat, quiet land opened up in front of us.

"Do you find these jobs by yourself?"

Buildings were few and far between now, and the few places we did see were all either karaoke bars or gigantic pachinko parlors. The surface of the road was still wet, covered in a layer of slush.

"The company's marketing rep arranged it."

"I thought you were self-employed? Isn't that what an independent is?"

"Yeah, I'm not a company man. It's just that it's really hard for private truckers to get their hands on a business plate—you know the green license plate you need if you want to drive for a business? I contract with a company for that."

It was five in the afternoon when he finished loading the tires.

Looking down from the overpass, I saw a few lights starting to come on along the wide riverbank. The rays of the setting sun bounced off the thin carpet of snow that still remained and off the clouds that hung in the west, making it seem as if the town were hovering in a field of orange. Wedged between the two areas of reflected light, stretching far into the distance, the sky gradually changed color from powder blue to ultramarine.

"Are we going to Niigata now?"

I wanted to be sure of where I was.

"Yeah."

"How will we get there? The Kan'etsu Expressway?"

"Nah, we take regular roads. We have to pay tolls and stuff ourselves."

"Oh."

"Hey, listen—you said you wanted to come for the trip, right?"

"What do you mean?"

"I'm married."

"Yeah, so what?"

So what? I tried to look as if I didn't care at all, feeling at the same time as if it were true, it really didn't bother me a bit, feeling at the same time as if I'd had a bucket of cold water thrown over me.

"Nothing. No problem."

"I noticed a pause there!" I cried in a childlike voice.

"It's just that I had someone following me around for a while. She was sort of like a stalker, I guess. Actually she's still following me. I was just thinking that it'd suck if you were like that. She's really intense, this woman."

". . . . ."

"What kind of work did you say you do?"

"Me? I write stuff."

"You're in a company, then?"

"No."

"So you're like me, an independent? You get paid for what you do?"

We passed Noda, then Kasukabe, and then I saw a sign that said "Kisai." The railway must not come out here, because there's no one place where the stores or houses cluster, they just keep going on and on, one here and one there, spread out. There was snow on the tin roof of a shabby old shop with a peeling, rusty sign over it, the writing on it done in calligraphy. Between the houses you could see fields where withered stalks jutted up out of patches of bare earth.

"What's the advantage of being an independent?"

"Well, you're not so tied down, first of all. Plus, until recently you could land some really juicy contracts. Of course, the economy's in bad shape right now, you know, so that kind of work is gone. I mean, say you've got a load of frozen tuna with packets of speed hidden in the entrails or something, all those jobs get handed over to free agents. With that kind of cargo there's no way they can put in a request with one of the big transport companies, but then, on the other hand, they don't want to risk handing the stuff over to some guy they don't know the first thing about. So they use their connections, you know, they go through friends of friends and whatever, trying to hunt down guys whose backgrounds are completely clear, people with fixed addresses and stuff, because unless they do it that way there's a chance they're gonna lose the goods.

They pack the drugs into the fish while the boats are still way out in the ocean, down to the south of Kyushu, and since the things are frozen solid, even the dogs they use at customs can't pick up the scent. So they get into the harbor, and unlike normal fish these have already got buyers waiting for them, so the brokers—these are yakuza I'm talking about here—they tell you they want the stuff taken into Tokyo as fast as possible, right into the Tsukiji fish market, so you get tolls for the highway and everything, five hundred thousand yen in hard cash. And when you get to Tsukiji, sure enough, there are buyers waiting."

"Do they tell you what's inside?"

"Oh yeah, they tell you. The terms are unusual, after all. And they say to you, 'Which do you want, five hundred thousand in cash or five hundred thousand worth of speed, you can have whichever you prefer.' I don't do speed, so I just take the cash."

"There are guys who take the speed?"

"Yeah. Down in Kyushu there were tons of truckers who were hooked. I mean, what do you expect? You're out driving all night, right?"

Okabe's face always had a very mild expression that made him seem like he'd be pretty quiet, but once you got him going he talked up a storm. Talking with him like this helped me forget the voices inside.

"When did you get married?"

"I guess it's been about three years."

"Do you have any kids?"

"Yeah, one."

"A boy or a girl?"

"Girl."

"Do you love her?"

"We're not really close. I don't get home much."

"I don't suppose you would, would you?"

"Not too often, no. I mean, most of the time I've got consecutive shipments, so I load up for the next trip as soon as I finish one and get ready to head out again."

"That's what you call it when you drive—a shipment?"

"Yeah, a shipment or a haul."

"If you're going round trip, that means you end up in Tokyo half the time, right? Where do you sleep when you go back to Tokyo?"

"The company has a place called the Driver's Lounge, but I hardly ever go there 'cause I feel more relaxed in the truck. This truck is my home."

"What do you call that place?" I pointed to the area behind the seats.

"That's the sleeper."

"Can I see what's it like to lie down?" I took off my shoes, then went back into the sleeper and stretched out. It was the first time I'd lain there full-length. "Wow, I can put my legs out all the way with no problem."

"I'd hope so. I can put mine out."

"How tall are you?"

"A little over six feet, I think."

"Wow, you're tall, aren't you?"

"Yeah, I guess I'm pretty tall."

"Hey, that woman stalking you knows, right? That you're married, I mean."

"She knows. I mean, she's been following me around for about ten years now, it's not like my getting married is gonna make her get off my back. She just has the wrong idea, that's the problem, and she's so convinced of things, like when she tells me she's the only one that really understands me and stuff. I just find it incredible that she can get so wrapped up in things. Guys like me, people who travel around to so many different places, we'll never be able to understand that kind of psychology, never. I mean, who knows, I might think this person here is the greatest, but maybe if I went up to Sendai there'd be someone I'd get along with even better than that, right? If you're a salary man and you're married and you're living in the sort of world where people think it's perfectly natural for you to stick with one woman, well, let's say you hit it off with some woman at work, too—people say you're having an affair. The thing is, that only holds if your home and your company are everything, if that's all there is in your world. I had to get a new mobile number like ten times or something, you know? And I use that phone to schedule all my work, so it was a huge pain in the ass, every time I changed it was a major hassle. And then the woman just totally plays dumb with me. 'What?' she'd say to me. 'What about your number? What do you mean, you're the one who gave it to me!' I mean, come on, there's no way in hell I'd give the fucking thing to her. And no matter how often we move, no matter where we go, one day she just shows up on our doorstep."

"How does she manage to find you?"

"She hires a detective. Once she called the company and told them some story, you know, said she was hoping to talk to me about my life-insurance policy because the term was almost up, was there any way she could get in touch with me and so on and so forth, that kind of thing; and then this asshole in the office decided to give her my mobile number, such a fucking jerk, Satoo is the guy's name. I mean, what the hell was he thinking? So I was like, 'Listen, why the hell would my term be up on my life insurance, just how old do you think I am, use your brain and tell her to fuck off, and since it's all your fault that I have to get my number changed, you're paying for it, you hear? And don't you ever give my number to anyone, never again, you hear, even if the police call!'"

"She's used the police, too?"

"No, she hasn't tried that one yet, but I figure that if you've tried the insurance company already, the police are probably next. Don't you think? Of course, the police could use their own information networks, and they wouldn't tell her anything anyway. Besides, I've got a past—they'd find me with no problem."

"Really? What did you do?"

"Eight counts of assault, two counts of possessing thinner . . . let's see, one count of selling thinner, two counts of blackmail. They all fall under the heading of what people call 'juvenile delinquency.' I was in a gang from my first year in high school right until I turned eighteen."

"You're what they call an ex-Yanky."

"Yeah, I guess you could say that."

"You don't really have that kind of a look, though."

"To tell you the truth, these gang fights are really none of their business, you know? They should just keep out of it. The only reason I ended up being charged was that I won; if I'd lost, I would've been the victim, right? That's what I told the police, anyway, blowing my own trumpet, so to speak, but it didn't work."

I found myself laughing. "It makes sense."

"Yeah, but when it's a kid talking it's just splitting hairs. If they were the kind of people who could understand that kind of thinking, I might not have been taken in in the first place. Oh yeah, I just remembered. There was a call from the fire station, too, once."

"The stalker? She said she was from a fire brigade?"

"I get a call from this ambulance, right, and they tell me she's slit her wrist, this woman, I mean, and they've got her and she's all covered in blood and everything but she says she won't let them take her until they get in touch with me. So I say to them, 'Put her on the line,' and when she came on I just yelled at her, 'Drop dead, you asshole!' and then I hung up."

"You hung up on a woman who'd slit her wrist?"

"Hold on! I'm the victim here, right? I am. Listen, if you really want to die, you take a bucket and you fill it with water and you soak your wrist in that after you cut it; that's how you do it. If you do it like that, you'll actually die."

"Were the two of you going out?"

"No way! We were never going out! . . . I gave her a ride once in the truck, that's all. I mean, she says she wants me to give her a ride, you know? What am I supposed to do? I kinda figured maybe it'd be enough for her if I just let her in the truck, maybe she'd get over it. Yeah, well that was a really stupid mistake on my part. Because while I was loading up the truck, you know what she did? She went through all my addresses and phone numbers and all that and copied down everything she could figure out. She got the number of the girl I was going out with then, she got my parents' number, she got all that, and then she used those as a springboard, you know, started making crank calls all over the place, it just went on and on and on. I called her parents and told them. I was like, 'Hey, listen, I've had to move so many times because of your daughter, maybe you could wake up and do something, huh?' And her father said, 'We're so sorry, we're so sorry, you can beat her up, you can do anything you like, it's fine with us, no problem,' that kind of thing, but come on. You know who gets in trouble if I pull a stunt like that? I do."

"Did you beat her?"

"Yes."

"With your fists?"

"Of course with my fists! Listen, the woman was chasing me around with one of those huge kitchen knives. I'd knock her down and she'd just keep chasing me, you know? When you have no sympathy for a woman, when it's a woman you really can't stand, she can be even worse than a man."

"Where did it happen?"

"At her house."

"What? Why the hell did you go to her house if you hated her?"

"The two can't coexist."

Huh?

"When I'm not driving the truck, there are times when I like to go home and relax. And when I'm like that, you just gotta leave me alone. That me is totally separate from this me, and the two of us can't coexist. There's one me that feels nice and relaxed when he gets home, and there's another me that feels nice and relaxed when he leaves the house and climbs up into this truck, and even though these are both the same person they're actually not the same person. The problem with this woman who's stalking me is that she's not content having just this me; she feels like she needs to destroy my other life, too. I mean, when I'm in the truck I don't mind doing some pretty wild things, but otherwise . . ."

"Was it scary, that time with the knife?"

Suddenly a car swerved in front of the truck, and Okabe hit the brakes.

"Fuck, that guy is a hazard."

When I'm having a conversation with someone, the voices become still, sedated. I change them into something like the blood flowing through my body.

The two can't coexist. I felt as if I'd heard something momentous.

Okabe talked up a storm, changing his tone to represent different people, doing it all with direct quotes. It was fascinating to listen to and I wanted to hear more, so I started drawing him out, getting him to keep talking.

The two can't coexist.

That's what Okabe had said. Did he mean that the person he is when he's in the truck and the person he is when he's not in the truck have become so different that they can no longer exist together, was that it? I kind of had the feeling that he'd had these two incompatible sides right from the beginning, and that he just drove his truck as a means of keeping them apart.

We drove up Route 17, taking some back roads along the way, and saw that this would take us pretty much straight up into Niigata; we'd pass through Saitama and Gunma on the way. Now that night had fallen, all the sounds and vibrations the truck made seemed louder and stronger. I rolled my window halfway down and stuck my face outside. There was still a little snow left by the side of the road, but the cold air outside felt dry. The wind played with my hair, hurting me. I tried calling out, but the sound was caught by the wind, broken up and instantly swept off into the distance, far behind the truck. Over in the driver's seat, Okabe was smiling. It was a very mild, well-mannered smile. I couldn't quite put my finger on it, but somehow I sensed a gap between his words and the way he spoke on the one hand, and his expression on the other. The gap made me want to know more about him, but at the same time it made me feel that I couldn't understand him.

I left the widow open a crack. After a while, I discovered that there was this zone inside the truck that resonated with the outside. The sounds of the engine and the wheels spinning and the body of the truck slicing through the air all merged to create a kind of hum—a noise like voices, like a large group of women singing in chorus. I heard the voices best when Okabe shifted gears, during the interval before the r.p.m. stabilized. It was a dissonance rather than a consonance, the sort of sound you get when adjacent tones collide, and it rose and fell almost imperceptibly. When you listen to a noise like that, the distortions start echoing into one another, making you feel peculiarly relaxed. But then I started getting the feeling that if those different sounds ever happened to end up in tune, I was going to hear something that had some kind of meaning. So I rolled up the window again. An uneasy, agitated feeling, a feeling like hairs standing on end, started to form in my chest. I began combing up the short fur that covered the seat and then smoothing it down again. I wanted to touch Okabe's naked skin, but since he was driving I couldn't. I ran my hand over the fur instead, smoothing it down. There was nothing to talk about, so I asked him about different things in the cab. There were two compartments, one over the driver's seat and one over the passenger's— he kept a long-sleeved shirt in the one on the driver's side and a short-sleeved shirt in the one on the passenger's side. You could recline the seats all the way, and if you needed to you could even push the gear lever down. The lever could be "reclined" just like the seats so it was called a "reclinable gear." I thought this was such a funny name for the thing that I found myself wanting to make a note of it. I groped around in my backpack, trying to find my notepad. It occurred to me then that this was second nature for me now, and I smiled wryly. I wasn't even on an assignment. Suddenly the whole thing seemed really funny, and I burst out laughing. Words. What are words, anyway?

Would I still smile if there were no words? Would
I have enjoyed things back when I had no words,
back when smiling was just a reflex? "You seem to be
having fun?" said Okabe. And for the first time I
realized that I was; right now, I really was having a
lot of fun. It's true, I'm always slow to notice what
I'm feeling. Earlier, when I realized that I wanted
Okabe and then immediately went and told him that
I wanted him—that had been a big event for me. As
I felt around in my backpack, my hand touched
something that wasn't my notebook, something
cold. It was my tape-recorder. I carried it around
with me so that I'd always be ready whenever anyone
called, no matter what time, no matter who.

"Welcome to Mount Kasho!" This was on a sign
with a map of the mountain. From the style of the
characters and the logo, you could tell this was a
sacred mountain, that it had a shrine on it somewhere.
I hadn't noticed when it happened, but at some point
the road we were on had started sloping gently
upwards. After a while, the red gateway to a Shinto
shrine appeared to our right, all lit up. It was huge.
The truck drove through it. As Okabe turned the
steering wheel, a much sharper incline came into view
in front of us. "He-e-ll-o-o, Mount Akagi," said Okabe.

"Is this still Route Seventeen?" I asked.

In reply to which Okabe grunted, "Three-five-
three." Then, "There's always traffic in Maebashi,
even really late at night, 'cause there are traffic
lights. So we're going over Mount Akagi instead."

Once more I looked at the map. Route 353 went around the southern side of the mountain. The shrine must be up at the peak, and the gateway we went under earlier must have been the outermost, the one that marks the entrance. The air down at sea level had been dry, but now that we were at a higher altitude I noticed tiny crystals drifting through the air, here and there, glittering. I kept gazing out at these crystals, and then after a while little white things started appearing, mixed in among the crystals. The white things soared though the air, weaving between the crystals as they dropped. And as I moved through these white flakes, it came to seem as if I were in a tube or a tunnel or something, cut off from the me I had been previously—here I was, moving within this space. Something before me leapt into action. The wipers had come on. It felt as if the meaning of the movement had seeped out from somewhere, that was how I understood it, and then gradually, ever so gradually, I began to remember my body.

. . . . it's snow.

The words appeared inside my mouth as if they had come bobbing up from an ancient layer of memory. I said them again: spoke the words clearly now, aloud. "It's snow." But then, as I continued staring out into the snow, the word "snow" started breaking apart—it disintegrated into s n o and w, and the force that had hung there between the four letters, the force that had held them all together, was gone now, and there was no way to retrieve it. I no longer understood why s n o and w had been linked in that way, or why this was the name for that white stuff falling in front of me. Oh, OK, I get it. It's because the things linking them have disintegrated, that's why they tumble down over everything— maybe. I touched my arms, reassured myself of their warmth, but that had nothing to do with the snow. I touched my cheeks, but they had nothing to do with the snow, and when I shifted my head to look at the person sitting next to me, I knew who he was, of course I knew him, but that still had nothing at all to do with the snow. Snow . . . has nothing to do with anyone. Just like there's no relationship between s n o and w. But then I started feeling as if maybe that wasn't really it—it's not that there's nothing between s n o and w, that's not it, the thing is that there's no end to the things between s n o and w, you can put them all together any way you want, and if you combine them totally randomly you end up with something white, pure white, just like you get white when you project the light of all three primary colors in the same place, and maybe that's what I'm seeing out there now, in front of me and below me and above me and behind me, those tiny white things that go on and on and on forever—maybe that's what that stuff is. I started to get the feeling that it was.

A strong horizontal force pushed me to the side. It felt as if everything inside me was about to be

tossed out, so I quickly wrapped my arms around my
body. The curve continued. Maybe it was like this—
maybe this is how the meaning of snow was lost? My
body kept being carried forward, that was all. Little
specks of light at the base of a vague, dimly glowing
slope of white. The colorful lights of the town
stretching on and on in a limitless expanse, not
crowded together but not particularly widely spaced
either, evenly distributed. Is that Maebashi? The
thought crossed my mind, but before sound could
exit my mouth it crumbled, it too split into pieces
and turned into flakes of white and fell; at the same
time it became particles of light that scattered below
me as I watched. I heard a noise in the distance. In a
place that resembled one of the white flakes tumbling
down around me, I heard a voice.

Is anyone listening?
Sure am—
One is close, one is far away.
Mishuku United—
Murasaki Number One here.
Ten-thirteen north of Tsukiyono, any snow?
Yeah, there's ice in Numata.
"Is that the CB?"

The voice emerged with no warning. The snow
was still falling, but I had emerged from the tunnel-
like mood I'd been in before.

"Yeah." Okabe's voice. "Tsukiyono is where you
get on and off the Kan'etsu Expressway. It's coming
up soon."

Northland Hokkaido . . .

This voice was softer, even more distant than the others. I could see why they call electro-magnetic waves by that name. The voices actually came in that form, rising and falling—they were waves in the most definite of senses. Waves absorb the influence of other waves and squirm into new forms; voices tremble.

"Man—now that's something you don't get too often!" Okabe shouted his surprise, his tone rising.

"What? What is it?"

"This guy's all the way up in Hokkaido. During the winter you almost never pick up signals from that far away. In summer you get things reflecting off the ionosphere and stuff, but . . ."

Little by little we were descending into lower altitudes. The lights of the town I'd seen earlier crept slowly up from the foot of the gentle slope, and it seemed to me that their creeping matched the tuning of the waves, and that in all the world only the two of us and the owner of that Hokkaido voice had any sort of link with one another: we were bound in a knot that spanned the darkness, you could feel the two points merging. That voice and the accompanying static were constantly being broken down into separate signals. Yet even so we were receiving them. Voices, the sounds we refer to as voices, are turned into something like Morse code. I focused on the sound as if I were trying to decipher a secret message embedded within it. I felt hot; my skin started tingling. My body felt hollow. I knew this feeling. Something deep within me was about to come bobbing up to the surface; something that had been lying submerged all along, held down by its own weight. What was it? When was it? When was that? It had seemed to be something I missed, something I feared . . .

"This is really weird," I said, almost to myself. "It's so far away, but it totally feels like it's closed into you."

Things were acting up inside me. I felt my insides sway again, just a little. I had no idea what was happening, and it was such an alarming sensation that I couldn't help myself, I reached out and put my hand on Okabe's shirt, felt his arm through the cloth. I wanted to feel skin. I wanted this inner swaying to stop. No, no, I didn't want it to stop. The CB stirred up some sort of noise inside me, but at the same time it made me terribly nostalgic. Something sways.

"Sometimes if the output is high it will sound closer than other CBs that really are nearby. Hokkaido is great in terms of location, so even under normal circumstances the waves travel very far. So if a guy in Hokkaido comes on and asks if anyone wants to break in, everyone, and I mean everyone, will hear it. So you get all these guys coming on at once, you know, 'Tokyo break!' and 'Chiba Bozo break!' and so on."

Chiba Bozo . . . ? Oh, Boso—the town.

"Only the stronger signals get picked up. So if the guy in Hokkaido comes on again and says,

'Tokyo, break go ahead,' well, you get tons of people in Tokyo, right, so only the stronger signals get picked up again, just like before."

My insides continued to sway. Maybe it was because we were on a mountain road with so many curves. Okabe took one of his hands from the steering wheel, laid it lightly on top of mine. Even when I closed my eyes it remained there under my eyelids—the long lines of streetlights coming and going at regular intervals, the white headlights on the other side of the road, the red tail-lights in front of us, all overlapping with the sideways sway of the curves. Then, just for an instant, the merest fraction of a second, the feel of his hand, his words, the mood I was in, everything entering my eyes, the vibrations—all these things were woven together, blended together so it all felt flat. "The thing is, the strong waves are always going to win out, you know," I was in some place that was nowhere in particular and I no longer had any particular form. "So there are times when you really can't tell," all these things piled up on top of the other like some heavy fabric, that's me. Hearing and seeing and being touched and touching, it's all mixed up, everything is equivalent, "whether they're close or strong." You can't divide it, no way to tell where you're feeling what. Everything gets replaced by tiny particles of information that flicker like lights. "At any rate there's not enough output on this end right now, so I can't talk back."

My eyes were open when I came to—I was still gazing at all the different lights. Finally I understood. I'd said the voice on the CB sounded "closed into you," and I'd meant that in a really abstract way, I'd been talking about hearing a sound, but he thought I was saying it sounded "close to you." I had been talking about consciousness, but he thought I was just talking about the lack of a sense of distance. But maybe the two were really the same. To be conscious of something is to have no sense of distance, to have the feeling that something is very close to you, to feel it moving closer to you, to feel that it has been closed into you. I blinked. The flashes that had unfurled behind my eyes weren't the same as the clusters of headlights that entered now through my pupils. The tiny, blinking particles of light I had seen before were gone.

By the time we reached the bottom of Mount Akagi, it had stopped snowing. There wasn't even any left on the ground.

As the road leveled out, a loud, static-filled voice jumped out at us.

Okabe took up his mike and responded. "Good evening, Narita Tour.

"This guy's a trucker, too," he told me, taking his thumb off the button on the mike. You can transmit only when you've got the button pressed down.

"Why do you call him Narita Tour?" I asked. Okabe replied that this was known as a "handle," a special nickname you use on the CB.

"But you said he's a trucker, right?"

"Yeah."

*Going up Seventeen, Minakami. Do you read me?
Ten-ten.*

This was someone with a very thick, heavy voice.
The sound the truck made as it thundered onwards
cut jaggedly through his speech.

"Merit Five. Going down Seventeen, Kamishiroi."

The look Okabe had on his face when he spoke
told me he was friends with the man on the other
end, whoever it was.

"Why is he called Narita Tour?"

"I don't know. Just 'cause this is all illegal—you
can't use your real name."

"What? Isn't this legal?"

Hey hey hey, Merit Five here, too, the voice was
speaking through a compound mixture of different
statics, then vanished with a crackle.

"It's legal up to point-five watts, I think that's
what it is—everyone over that is illegal. This baby
can do two kilowatts."

"How much is point-five watts?"

The conversation continues automatically.

"Enough to get you nowhere. When conditions
are bad it won't go any farther than the transceiver,
just the transceiver, that's it. So everyone puts in a
booster, you know, to get more power."

"How many different kinds are there?"

"Well, there's personal and there's amateur."

"Amateur is what you call ham, right?"

Man oh man. Lotta snow in Tokyo this year.

Then, before Okabe could reply, the guy on the other end came on again:

Seriously, it snowed again!

"'CQCQ, this is blah blah.' That's ham, right?"

"Yeah."

This morning all the electrical stuff died on me, man what a pain in the ass that was, it was just crazy. The lights are down and the heater's down and the tachometer's down . . . nothing else I could do, so I took the highway.

"What does CQ stand for, by the way?"

Of course, with electric stuff like that, all the problems disappear the second you take it in to get repaired. That's how it goes, man.

"Someone was telling me it comes from English, it's an abbreviation of the words 'seek you.' Though I've also heard that it stands for 'come quick.' It's a code you use when you're trying to find someone in a crowd."

I was thinking, Yeah, better take her into the Mitsubishi shop tomorrow, but of course the problem's gone now . . . Go figure.

"Huh, I didn't know Mitsubishi made trucks."

"Mitsubishi Fuso."

Yeah, when the electrical stuff busted on mine it turned out the key was getting stuck between the engine and the accessories positions. Kept happening all the time. Dunno, maybe that's a problem in Isuzus or something. I put in a claim and got it fixed and all, but it's not like we're trucking for a company or something, you know. If we ain't on the road, we ain't eating.

"Is that Mitsubishi? I thought Fuso was the name of a company."

"It's Mitsubishi."

Man, that sucked, that really sucked!

"Is this an Isuzu?"

"Yeah . . . Hey, Narita Tour, they got signs around Akagi saying there's some Nakamoto coming. Stopping the falling rocks, looks like. Better move your ass."

"Nakamoto?"

"Construction."

What, so the left's gonna go?

"You only use CB?"

"CB's the most fun."

"In what way?"

Yeah.

OK. Arigato, guy.

Hello, hello, do you re-e-a-d me?

A second voice from the speaker.

"You cut in on other signals, you get cut off by other signals. It's all about power, who wins, who loses. You don't get that kind of negotiating with the ham, and besides with the ham you get all these idiots doing the sort of talking they might as well do on the phone."

Hey there. Listen, I'm in a rendezvous with Narita Tour right now.

"A rendezvous?"

"When you have three or more you call it a network."

OK, buddy. I read you loud *and* clear.

"Who's that in the background, the ones who are all scrambled?"

"Other channels. They cut in on you like this if they're strong. These people aren't that close. It's just that their signals are really strong. Mine probably isn't cutting in on theirs."

Haven't bought a porn mag yet today? Man, what a drag.

This was the owner of the second voice.

Ha ha ha.

This guy seems pretty funny.

"It's always like this. Like they're drunk or something."

We drove on for a while, and finally up ahead I saw a sign for Tsukiyono blink on, just once. Okabe flicked on his indicator and we headed towards the rest area. Instead of turning into the parking lot he drove into the lane that led back out to the highway. He brought the truck to a stop over on the left side. He turned off the CB. Apart from the sound of the engine idling, to which my body had grown accustomed, it was silent. There was a net of green wire with a shallow stream running underneath it: the nearly full moon was reflected, shattered, on the water's surface. The mountain began just beyond the narrow bed of the stream. I listened, but I couldn't even hear the trickling of the water. The snow heaped on the rocks was orange from the streetlight, bluish yellow from the moon, and white. The water flowed among the rocks and the snow, making small turns this way and that. Okabe seemed to have stopped talking only a few seconds ago, but already he was asleep.

The exchange that had taken place over the CB had replayed itself in the silence. Suddenly it struck me that it was like it was a written dialogue, broken up by quotation marks. When you're using a CB, you can only transmit stuff as long as you've got the button pressed down; and as long as you're transmitting, the other person's voice can't reach you. It's the same when conversation is represented as direct speech: as long as one person is filling the "   ", no one else can say anything. That's how it goes, that's the rule. You never have two people talking at once; you never have different statements or stories getting mixed up. It's not possible to express that using quotation marks. The speaking subject changes with each new quotation—you skip from one to another. So when one person is speaking the others are just waiting, keeping quiet. Of course, that's not how it is in reality, it's just how people have agreed to do things. When you're listening to the CB, you get the feeling its little speaker is giving you the vibrations of the air, the sound of the air, and that's not something you can express in "   ".

The mix of static and voices kept playing on and on in my head.

The glow of the moon and the streetlight streamed in from the right and left, dissolving into one another, tinting Okabe's face with gradations of blue and orange.

Beyond his face, it was starting to snow again.

"Weren't you afraid of the knife? The time she chased you?"

"Nah, that doesn't scare me. I'm used to knives."

"What do you mean? Why?"

"Oh, you know. I played around with them when I was a kid."

"Did you have one in high school?"

"A knife? I didn't really carry one around or anything, but when I went to gang meetings there was this guy who always had a sword, an actual samurai sword. Every so often he'd let people catch a glimpse of it."

"What, you mean a real one? A real Japanese sword?"

"As real as it gets. If you're in a gang—well, basically when you graduate from a gang, you end up in an actual criminal organization, see? Some guys even had pistols."

"You weren't interested in belonging to a group like that, were you?"

"I was in one."

"What?"

"I was way down at the bottom, just a member-in-training. I did my residence and everything."

"Your residence?"

"You go to stay at a boss's place for about a week and he makes you do stuff for him. That's supposed to train you. After you get assigned actual work—you answer the phone at headquarters, go around to check up on the snack bars and stuff. When your pager bleeps you go to whatever snack bar it is and get money out of some rowdy drunk, that kind of stuff.

"Well, you start out easy, tell him it'll be OK, he just has to pay up. You slip a business card out of his wallet. Meanwhile, you take pictures of him from somewhere out of sight, get shots of him tangled up with a girl. That, right there, is enough for a hundred thousand. Then . . . well, these jerks who go to bars and get drunk and then start going on about this and that and whatever, they've all got something going on, so next you figure out what it is, use a detective agency and get pictures and stuff, you know, then tell him, 'Hey, man, it's up to you! But you know, I'd say we oughta just keep this between you and me, huh, 'cause actually I know where your parents live, too, where was it again, I think it was . . . ' and stuff. 'Hell, this isn't extortion, there's no fuckin' extortion going on here, just five hundred thousand will be fine, huh? Five hundred thousand, that OK?' You don't want to hound the guy too much. Other than that, I guess you do a little of this and a little of that, collecting debts, collecting on bills people haven't been able to pay, stuff like that; say there's five million yen and you collect five million yen, you get a million or so. Let's see, what else is there . . . yeah, you go get a girl, one of these high school girls you see around, girls on paint thinner and stuff, you get one of them and you put her to work in the snack bar and introduce her to your boss, make her his woman. You know, it's pretty dull when you're down on the bottom."

"When did you quit?"

"I ditched that in less than two years. I'm the kind of guy who loses interest in stuff pretty quickly, you know, so all that yakuza stuff just got boring. After that I was a manager at this *hotetoru* in Uguisudani. There's this guy over in Okachimachi, a real big operator in the underworld, Mr. Sakamoto is his name. I went and worked under him, did that stuff for a while, but then I got sick of that, too. I was so bored I started getting sloppy, and I got nabbed."

"What for?"

"*Hotetoru.*"

"How did that work?"

"Customers see your flyers and call up, right? You know, you see those flyers stuck up in phone booths and stuff, that's the kind of thing I'm talking about. So you answer the phone and you say, 'OK, so what kind of girl are you looking for? Well then, I'm gonna bring her to this coffee shop'—in Uguisudani we used a place called the Half Moon. So I'd tell him, 'I'm gonna bring her to the Half Moon, so go and wait for us there. She's got hair that's more golden than gold, so you'll be able to find us with no problem,' and then we go and meet the guy. 'Wow, she's great, just great.' 'Great, great, but I'm afraid I'm gonna have to ask you to pay in advance, and you gotta be sure to stick to the time limit, OK. If she's not back in two hours, I'm coming in, OK, so be sure that doesn't happen. And if you get caught, do us a favor and cook up some kind of story: tell 'em she's your girlfriend. The thing to do is to tell 'em you picked her up somewhere, that's how you ended up lovers, that's what you gotta do.'"

It was the first time I'd heard of this system.

I'd done some reporting on the sex industry, and I knew that most of the time girls would be contacted by the office and they would go to whatever location they were told to visit. The customer would have no idea what sort of place had sent the girl out or what sort of people were behind it. The office would be contacted by phone whenever somebody went over the time limit, but the basic assumption was that the people in the office would welcome any extra income they could get. Maybe the set-up Okabe had just described was peculiar to the organization he was in. Or maybe that was how pimps used to do things in the old days.

There was some kind of lump in my chest. Something unsayable.

"I got sick of it all, you know, so I started with something else, and then the guy underneath me got nabbed. After that, Mr. Sakamoto asked me if I'd be interested in running a snack bar for him, but I was so bored by then that I just told him no. I guess it was then that I started thinking maybe I ought to try and find some kind of job, you know, doing some legitimate work."

"You were about nineteen then?"

"Yeah."

"You said you were a building contractor first?"

"That was right after I graduated. No, actually that must've been eighth grade, that's when it was— which is why I never graduated from high school. Of course, there was reform school. I graduated from that."

"You didn't sell speed or anything?"

"No, I never got into that."

"And you didn't do speed?"

"Oh, I've done it, did it about twice, I guess, but I was still sniffing thinner, you know, I was still just a kid then so it didn't really do much for me, it didn't move me or anything, I was just doing thinner all the time, getting high on that."

"You liked sniffing thinner?"

"I don't know if I'd say I liked it or not—I wonder. I guess it was more that I couldn't stop, you know, not that I really liked it that much or anything. And when you're in high school you can make money with that stuff. You sneak into a rubber factory or something at night and make off with two or three four-gallon containers and you can sell it for about a million yen."

"You've sure done a lot of different stuff, huh?"

"I wanted to give it all a try. You don't know until you give it a try, you know, whether it's interesting or not so interesting or what. For me, it was a lot harder to understand guys who just do a little of something and then pull out immediately. I mean, if you want to know what I think about all that now, I think sniffing thinner is pretty dumb, actually, but I'm only able to say that 'cause I've done it, right? Every so often a hostess at a bar or someone will come up to me with a problem, tell me they want to talk things over. They come and they say, 'Listen, my kid brother's kind of hooked on thinner, you know. You think you can do anything for him?' Or, "Listen my husband got taken in for doing speed, you know. Think you can do anything for him?" But the thing is I understand that feeling: it feels so incredible you just want to go on doing it forever, I know that, and besides, if I were the kind of guy who could actually do anything for people like that I figure someone would've been able to do something for me some-where along the way."

"What else have you tried?"

"Oh, I don't know, not much. I wasn't much different from everyone else."

"Trust me, you're pretty different!"

"I just did what I wanted, that's all. I tried what everyone wants to try."

"I doubt most people want to try being a yakuza."

"Then why does everyone go to see these gangster movies and stuff? If people really weren't interested in things like that, then you wouldn't have these movies, and even if you did no one would go to see them. Say you made a movie called *Let's Learn How to Solve Mathematical Equations!*—who the hell do you think is gonna go and watch that? No one would even think about going, right? Everyone goes for things that interest them, right? So I went for things that interested me. I'm not all that different."

A weak snow was still falling.

There was almost no wind at all, and the snowflakes themselves were so light that instead of dropping in straight lines, cleaving the air, they circled as they fell. As soon as we got onto the bypass that headed over the north side of Niigata City, signs for various intersections started appearing, regularly spaced. At times like this I instinctively start counting. It's not like counting is going to help anything; it's just a habit. I'd counted the third turn-off, for Sakuragi, when the winter sun started slowly climbing into view. The light bounced off the thin curtain of clouds overhead, splintering off in all directions so that the whole sky sparkled like a silver dome, and it was even brighter than when the sky was clear. We turned off the bypass at the seventh intersection—a place called Hitoichi. The sky here was as clear as it could be, but still the snow continued to dance. Just a small change in time or place and the weather is completely different.

This whole area was arranged in a grid, just like a Go board: here and there on the grid were square clusters of squat factories, all equipped with the same type of ventilation duct. The blocks were separated by roads. You could see a long way, and there was no one in sight. The few vehicles we passed were all car transporters. The sky was blue and clear, but the snow piled up along the side of the road had hardly melted; it looked like it would be there until spring, and it was dirty from the exhaust smoke and the clumps of pavement torn up by snow tires.

Okabe stopped the truck in front of a furniture factory and we closed the curtains. The inside of the cab was now ruled by a gray like the color of a windless, snowy, slightly overcast sky shortly before sunrise. Apart from the rain, we couldn't tell what the weather was like outside. I eyed my watch: 10:30 a.m. Okabe glanced at the clock on the dashboard. In the sleeper he embraced me, then all of a sudden he pushed his hand in from the side, under my panties. The fabric twisted into a rope. Okabe's fingers passed quickly over the soft part of me he had now exposed and sank inside. No matter when it happened, my body was always ready the moment he touched me. Only this time my heart and mind both responded by withdrawing. It happened so fast I didn't have time to bridge the gap between what he was doing now and the gentleness with which he had embraced me the previous day. My arms and shoulders stiffened, making us fall out of sync, and Okabe fell asleep. Suddenly he felt unbearably heavy in my arms. I couldn't fall asleep so easily.

My consciousness dissolved and returned again; this cycle was repeating several times, and then there was a knock at the window. Okabe got up and

drove the truck around, a sleepy look on his face.
Someone from the factory must have come to let
him know it was time to get to work.

The furniture factory's loading dock was the
same height as the bed of the truck. You open the
doors of the trailer, swinging them out from the
middle and folding them around on either side, then
back the truck up to the loading dock so that the two
are perfectly aligned. That way you can carry the
cargo in with no problem. Okabe put on his boots
and went to start working. I asked him if it'd be
alright if I went out with him, then left the truck.
The temperature was still fairly low. I stood under
the eaves of the factory, warming my cold hands as I
watched Okabe. His arms stretched out to grab a
wooden frame. Maybe it's a door frame, I don't know.
Come to think of it, he told me he was delivering
doors when we first met. He would stack two on his
shoulders with his head sticking up in the middle,
then carry them out, supporting them by applying
equal pressure with both arms. Again and again he
went through these motions. I found myself struck
by the self-evident fact that humans and furniture
are not at all the same. There is no intersection
between us and furniture. That's what I keep
thinking—the thought enters my head as a phrase,
like some sort of proposition. People are soft, wood
is hard. Suddenly it occurs to me that I could probably beat someone to death if I used one of those
wooden door frames; it wouldn't take more strength

than I have. A vision of massacre drifted up in my mind, and at the same time a vision of rooms being completely and utterly destroyed—rooms furnished with the pieces that the men were now carrying out. These scenes arose without my wanting them; they were unrelated to my will—they burned themselves into my mind in a single blast, like a flash of a strobe light. I had a hard time making my body move. The visions had come in such a sudden bright burst that I couldn't discern any of the details. Okabe and the people from the factory carefully loaded the furniture, all packed up in protective cardboard, into the bed of the truck.

Finally I managed to turn my head and look away. Except for a few places where the wheels of numerous trucks had bitten into the earth, the ground was covered with a thin layer of snow, and it was very bright. Fine flakes still danced down against the backdrop of blue sky. I turned my head again and watched Okabe. I watched his body move. This time it was a sound that came drifting up, all on its own. There were the things I saw, and then there were these different sounds on top of them. It was like a movie when you get a monologue or some kind of narration or something running through a scene to which it has no obvious relation. Okabe was quite near by, and yet he seemed cut off from me— it was like watching a movie projected on a screen. The blue and white that made up the background competed in the brightness of their exposure,

becoming dots; they started to seem flat. I began to
hear words, a voice I had encountered a short while
before, exactly the same as earlier, dubbed over the
image of Okabe's working body.

*"I'm gonna bring her to the Half Moon, so go and wait
for us there. She's got hair that's more golden than gold, so
you'll be able to find us with no problem,"* and then we go
and meet the guy. *"Wow, she's great, just great." "Great,
great, but I'm afraid I'm gonna have to ask you to pay in
advance, and you gotta be sure to stick to the time limit,
OK. If she's not back in two hours, I'm coming in, OK, so
be sure that doesn't happen."*

Okabe moves. The sky is clear, but the snow is
still falling.

If I sat up a little I could see the Tone River.

Now we were heading for Tokyo. Just over the
border between Gunma and Saitama prefectures, in
a town named Fukaya, Okabe had put his seat back
to take a nap. The soft curves of his upper body
stuck out at an angle from the seat; that part of him
was in the sleeper. His shoulders were rising and
falling at regular intervals. The neon lights of the
large, apparently not terribly popular video arcade
where the truck was parked kept changing the color
of the shadow on his cheek. A metallic-looking ridge
kept appearing, then vanishing. Only three cars in
the parking lot. I couldn't sleep the way he could. It
was just me now, so I was lying there listening to the
tape I'd made, using my earphones. I knew by now
that it took more than a little to rouse Okabe.

Transcribing tapes is part of my work, and I'd
figured that by now I was pretty used to hearing my
own voice. The thing is, there's a difference between
talking with a certain theme in mind and just chatting
about things the way you usually do. I hadn't realized
how slowly I spoke when I was just chatting.

*"I'm gonna bring her to the Half Moon, so go and wait
for us there. She's got hair that's more golden than gold, so
you'll be able to find us with no problem," and then we go
and meet the guy. "Wow, she's great, just great." "Great,
great, but I'm afraid I'm gonna have to ask you to pay in
advance, and you gotta be sure to stick to the time limit,
OK. If she's not back in two hours, I'm coming in, OK, so
be sure that doesn't happen."*

Rewind.

Part of it is that Okabe talks so fast that he makes
me sound slow by comparison. But what's the difference—why does he talk so quickly, and why am I so
slow? He says about three times more than I do in
the same time—I get the feeling that if you wrote it
all down, he would end up having three times as
much writing as I would, all crammed into the same
space. Okabe isn't like me, he doesn't waste his time
saying, "Uhh" and "Hmm" and thinking and stuff;
he just talks. Earlier, when I'd come across the tape
recorder I use for interviews and asked him, "Hey, is
it OK if I tape you?" he hadn't minded a bit, he
hadn't even asked why, and the fact that he was
being recorded hadn't made him change his tone. I
think with people like Okabe—people who talk a
lot—the thing is that they're not working under the

assumption that what they say will be preserved.
Words exist only where they're spoken: they emerge
in a stream and they stop and that's all there is to it,
they end with the moment. Whereas I start out from
the assumption that the things I say will remain, so
I choose my words very carefully, and so I speak more
slowly, and because I speak slowly I say less . . . I'm
sure that's it. And yet, even so, whenever I go back
and reproduce my conversations with people, when
I play them back on tape, I find it hard to understand what I'm saying.

*"If she's not back in two hours I'm coming in, OK, so be
sure that doesn't happen."*

I'm extremely fond of this section: I keep rewind-
ing it to listen again and again. I wonder if maybe I
could have been a prostitute if I'd had a man like him
to watch out for me. I wouldn't want to do it, but he'd
take me by the hand and lead me to the Half Moon
and I'd go off with the customer, I'd give the guy a
condom straight away, just as Okabe had instructed
me to do, and then I'd lie there for two hours but no
longer with the sweaty, oily skin of the man pressing
down on top of me. I would be nothing but a mucous
membrane; I would extinguish my heart.

I rewound the tape, and as the lines I wanted to
hear began playing again for the umpteenth time I
felt something like a knot that linked certain memories I had all but forgotten forming once again
within me. I had been hit. I had been hit in eighth
grade, by a teacher. This was in Tokyo, and he taught
Japanese, but he had a very strong north-eastern

accent, totally obvious, as showing up in places that weren't supposed to have them, and he spent most of the class pointing to all the different conjugative suffixes and making us say them one after the other: "sa-row" irregular conjugation, "ra-row" irregular conjugation, all of them in sequence. He was a short, bald man. His eyes were as narrow as pieces of string, but the edges of his eyelids were so fat and clear that you could see the pink membranes on the undersides, almost as if the eyelids themselves had been peeled back.

When you keep repeating verb conjugations they start to seem like some weird sort of spell, and you end up forgetting what they're supposed to mean. You couldn't really say we did anything in class, there was no content, and yet there was always a strange feeling of tension. The only thing we learned was how to let our eyes swim vaguely through space and thus escape being called on.

It was an accident. A momentary loss of balance on my part just happened to catch the teacher's eye—I suppose that's what happened. The stumpy man knew perfectly well that he was the butt of everyone's jokes, so it took only one person who had stopped paying attention to make him feel as if the whole world was ignoring him. That was his sickness. "Hayawaka!" he said. "Stand up!" and so I stood, and then all of a sudden he whipped the back of his hand across my cheek. I didn't slap the teacher back; I didn't even cry.

The air had frozen; it wasn't the sort of space where it would even be possible for me to raise my voice. I felt reality slipping away, that was all. I suppose I must have decided to take the most passive approach, must have made up my mind that since I'd look bad no matter what I did I wouldn't do anything at all, so I became something that breathed, that was all I was, like an ion membrane automatically exchanging substances for other substances; I simply inhaled and exhaled, inhaled and exhaled, and you know, maybe that was when it happened, maybe that was when I first started hearing the voices.

After that, whenever I had to recite the "sa-row" and "ra-row" conjugations there would be this voice speaking inside me, keeping just a little ahead of me. The voice remembered the conjugations for me, remembered them so I wouldn't have to, and since doing those conjugations made me want to throw up, I would let it say the conjugations in my place. I'm not the one reciting these things, I didn't give in to you, I'm not gonna remember these stupid conjugations just because you want me to. And then something even worse happened. In ninth grade I had the same Japanese language teacher for home economics.

I informed my parents that my teacher had hit me for no reason. My idea was to get the matter raised at the board of education, to launch a frontal attack, see that he was sanctioned according to the rules, but my mother just said I must have done something bad, she wouldn't listen to a word I said, she didn't listen, she blamed it all on me. The strange tension in that classroom wasn't something you could see— it was a feeling that wrapped itself around your skin, something that hung in the air, and the task of communicating the strangeness of it was well beyond a fourteen-year-old like me—but even so I staunchly refused to back down, kept insisting until my mother came out and said very clearly:

"Do you have to be such an embarrassment?"

From then on she always asked the same question when she noticed something strange in the way I was acting: she'd say, "You haven't gone and done something to make your teacher hit you again, have you?" School was no fun and I couldn't relax when I was at home. Without even realizing it, I had started building up a collection of knives in my drawer. The knives were lovely. Especially the ones that curved inwards ever so slightly and then became broader again near the point; I worshipped that shape. I would let them rest vertically against my skin; sometimes I would let them lie flat. They would never hurt me, but they would tear through anyone who hurt me, anyone who tried to hem me in. These silver, glinting blades were precisely what I needed to fight off the silky, inexplicable feeling of entrapment that surrounded me. It seemed as though I might get stuck to the background, might become ambiguously united with it, and so I wanted

to take those silver, glinting blades and use them to
carve out the line of my own perimeter.

Only much later did I put my anger into words.
And when I told my mother how much I had been
hurt at the time, her reply—which is to say her
excuse—was so self-serving and deceptively kind
that I could hardly believe it. "You've got to understand, when you're a parent with a child in high
school, for all practical purposes it's as if your kid
were being held hostage by the school. That's just
how it works." The way she phrased it was common
enough—it wasn't that my mother was particularly
cruel or anything—but the fact that it was so common
just made it more frightening. It wasn't the living
bodies of their children that parents wanted to protect but something else. I mean, if they really believe
all this crap, then they're the ones who are crazy,
they're all raving mad, them and their friends, all
those people parading around like bundles of good
sense with clothes on, my classmates' moms and
dads, they're all, all, all, every one of them, raving
mad. They keep it concealed under a layer of ordinary
skin but underneath that they're crazy. I wanted to
peel away the skin and expose what was hidden
underneath. So what if they're in the majority, who
cares? That sure as hell doesn't prove that they're
right, not by any means. If the majority were right,
then war would be right, too.

"How long are you going to keep dragging up
these old things?" said my mother, and that was the

end of it. Well, you didn't listen when I said it back then, did you? Just when am I supposed to say it, then, huh? I would have pointed out how quickly adults forget when they've trampled on someone else's rights, except that by then I was an adult, too.

"If she's not back in two hours I'm coming in, OK, so be sure that doesn't happen."

I imagine myself being protected by Okabe. The customer takes out ropes and stuff and I plead with him, "Please, listen, you can't do anything dangerous. If you leave any cuts or bruises on my body or anything like that the office will do terrible things to you," but the man shows no sign that he's inclined to stop. OK, it's just for two hours, that's all there is in my head, and I pull together all the little pieces of myself that are drifting here and there around the room, focus every nerve in my body in an effort to make the man feel good during the brief period of time we're going to be together, I show him what I can do, concentrate as hard as I can, blow jobs and all that, and so we end up going a bit over two hours and Okabe comes in and I tell him, "This guy was going to do terrible things to me," and then Okabe goes through the customer's things, yells at him for having broken the rules: "This isn't extortion, buddy, we've got a perfectly legitimate right to do this," he says. "You're the one who didn't abide by the rules, you're the one who wanted to abuse this poor woman." Okabe's a pretty big guy, there aren't many people who could beat him in a fight, there's no longer any need for me to be afraid. He pats my head. We go back to the office and have lunch. We have some tea and sweets. "That was a pretty tough job, huh?" he says, and pats my head again.

Back then I didn't think I'd be able to get by if I left home, but as a matter of fact that wasn't true. I was extremely young and youth didn't cost a thing, and youth is something you can sell. I bet I could have made a living selling my body the way teenage girls do now, with no pimp or anything, but even now, even if I were still in my teens, I lack the courage to do that. I can't manage to forget the possibility that I'd be raped or tormented or killed. So without a guy like Okabe protecting me, I never would have been able to work as a prostitute. If I'd known about this *hotetoru* system back then, maybe I wouldn't have had to stay there in that rotten place, but then maybe sooner or later a day would have to come when I'd have regretted running away from school; maybe I'd have spent my days being cheated out of the money I'd earned some pimp; maybe that's how things would have been. But then on the other hand even when I was at school I never had the feeling that I was alive, and my own parents were bleeding the life force out of me. There was no way I could escape that place. I think the feeling I had then, the sense of being unable to get away, must have been similar to what an insect feels when it's being killed, like what a herbivore feels after its carotid artery has been severed, ever so precisely, by a predator: they say the lives of insects are nothing but an effect of the interaction between electricity and certain chemicals and that when an insect is killed some other chemical reaction makes it go numb so that in fact it feels good, and they say that when the herbivore gets its throat bitten through by the carnivore a flood of endorphins is released so that it feels no agony when it dies. There is a certain perverted nerve that feels a vaguely nostalgic pleasure in death, in the passage into death. Maybe once that nerve begins to function you become unable to run away.

As soon as the word "endorphins" entered my mind it gave me a link to a different site and I found myself wondering, all of a sudden, whether self-induced vomiting might not be a way of simulating death. As a matter of fact, the feeling I get when I do it is sort of like the strange sense of numbness that came over me when I was slapped by that teacher. I stood there thinking that the humiliation wasn't really humiliation, that the pain wasn't really pain, and gradually the area where I'd been hit started to tingle, and I stopped being able to tell whether it hurt or whether I liked it. I felt such loathing for the *me* that liked it that I wanted to throw up; I couldn't believe this *me* was really *me*; I felt myself breaking away from myself. But in order to confirm that this was really happening I would have to experience something extreme, something similar to the slap. Maybe that was why I started collecting knives. The fastest way to forget my hatred was to sleep, so I started spending more time lying alone in my bed. I would lie down and my breathing would slow to the very lowest possible rate, I would feel my own flesh trembling with the beating of my heart. Starting from around fourteen or fifteen I would often lie as if I were dying even as I lived, asleep with my eyes wide open.

Ever since then, I've had trouble viewing my memories as my own. The more important or desperate the situation, the more objective my stance toward the memory of it becomes. No matter where I am, I find myself unable to feel that I am 100 percent there. But I was always affable with others, I made sure to do the things I was supposed to do. There were no ruptures.

I don't talk about myself, I only listen.

I opened the curtain a little and looked out. I cleared the mist on the window with my hand. A large, red moon had risen low over the river.

At Toda, we took the southern ramp on to the Shuto Expressway.

We would be on the Ringway in another twenty minutes. The quantity of light in the sky increased explosively, and all of a sudden Tokyo was before us. Countless microbes squirmed and murmured, glowing in their transparent shells. The truck continued moving forwards, slashing through the heart of the swirl of white light, but no matter how far we went it never ended.

"Tokyo's incredible, it really is," said Okabe. "I bet none of these people have any idea that there are guys like me out here, do they? That there are people zooming along out here this time of night, whacked from lack of sleep."

"Are you telling me it's always like this?"

"What do you mean? Always like what?"

"Is napping the only sleep you ever get on the road?"

"Yup."

"That's not just when you're busy?"

"It's not just when I'm busy."

It was midnight and we were zooming down the Shuto Expressway at seventy miles an hour. All those different landscapes I'd seen earlier dissolved into white light in the rush of speed. Unrelated scenes rose before me, connected by the speed, creating hundreds of thousands of pasts and presents. Not a single one of the scenes was now, but none of them was unrelated to now. The landscape before me now will be gone in an instant. And like a field over which all these scenes had been scattered, Tokyo surrounded me, glowing. It was the first time I had ever felt nostalgia for the city, and I realized how speed and time change the landscape, and it was so extreme it was almost violent, and I almost cried.

"Being a trucker would suck if you were an insomniac, huh?"

"I bet it'd be great. You don't have to sleep, right? More profit."

"Insomnia isn't that kind of disease. You can't sleep even when your body is so tired you can't take it—that's what insomnia is."

"I've always gone and done the stuff I wanted to, and, you know, being an insomniac is one thing I never really wanted to try."

"Lately the CB's getting on my nerves, I might take it out."
"Why? Isn—"
The 120-minute tape flipped over.
". . . ave it?"
The shore of Tokyo Bay, 1 a.m., Toyosu, Koto Ward. We were at a warehouse close to the construction site, waiting for morning. We were back in the same city, but this wasn't a residential area like the place where we had met.

"Don't get me wrong, I'm pretty big on it myself, you know. I mean, I go right on doing it even when I get fined and all, so I must get a kick out of it, huh? The thing is, they keep asking me to join the leadership of the club, you know, since I've been doing it so long. Naturally I know tons of guys." "Why don't you do it?" "Too much trouble. The people at headquarters are all yakuza, see; it'd just be a lot of trouble. They like getting people together, organizing get-togethers at hot springs and stuff, you know. Awful, just awful. 'Hey, buddy, how're things up north, huh?' 'Nothing much doing, same as always—what the hell do you expect? We're not like you right-wing guys, after all.' I borrow the company station wagon or something, right, and then there are all these assholes driving up in Mercedes. Wearing these shiny suits and all, and I'm wondering, What the hell is going on in your minds? 'What kind of vehicle do you usually drive, huh?' 'Tractor trailer.' 'So

you're just a trucker, right?' 'Yeah.' I mean, come on. Man, I can't stand guys like that, these fuckers going around like they're big shots. Then in summer you gotta go swimming with the whole club, you know, and you get all these guys with their families and couples and all that, and you gotta stand up in front of them with the mike and talk, you know, that's what you do when you join the leadership."

We were parked in a huge, flat space with nothing but rows of warehouses, and there was no sign of anything living anywhere I looked. We'd turned in through one of the many open gates that lined the highway, then driven through a gigantic gymnasium-like building with beams running around it, way up high. Once we got outside again there were no tall objects to block our view, nothing at all, and the sky opened out over our heads like a dome. Out here there were four trucks of the same make and two cabs with empty flatbeds behind them, all parked in a row, one beside the other. Maybe the drivers were sleeping inside; you couldn't tell from outside. About twenty yards ahead, directly in front of us, the mass of reclaimed land came to an end, the concrete dropped off at a right angle, and there, suddenly, was the ocean—this was obvious from a yellow sign sticking out over the road. And yet, except for those places where it reflected lights glowing in the distance, it was impossible to distinguish the heavy black liquid from the land. A clear, white, full moon hung in the deep, navy-blue sky, giving off just enough light to fill the darkness between the scattered lights. The CB and the radio were both

off—it was quiet. The hum of my tape player
skimmed lightly over the murmur of the idling
engine.

*"Why do the yakuza get involved?" "Oh, you know,
you've only got a limited number of channels, right, so it's
all about fighting for territory, and of course CB gets even
more competitive than the rest—it's totally a question of
who's got the most power. Whenever you've got illegal stuff
going on and there's competition between different factions,
any place where force rules the game, they're definitely
gonna show up, that's what yakuza are all about. They're
like leeches." "That's why it ends up being a club, then. Are
there any people who are mixed up in this stuff who don't
belong to the club?"*

I found myself glancing at the door to make sure
it was locked, though there was also a small part of
me that felt fear at being shut inside this small cab.

*"No one using a CB. You can't have a CB unless you
belong to some sort of club somewhere." "Come to think of
it, I don't really understand this stuff with the channels."*

I don't know if it was just because I wasn't used
to it or what, but for some reason when we'd been
moving for a long time I had trouble convincing
myself that the *me* at each of the places we stopped
was connected to the person I had been before. The
scenery would change completely in an hour, and
whenever we stopped at one of these places I had
the sense that I was cut off, locked in the present
place and time. The only place I could rely on was the
truck. Sitting inside, I could see why some truckers
like to decorate their rigs. Those trucks you see with
the gaudy exteriors and the peculiarly dainty, cutesy

interiors made sense to me now. Once you're on the road, the scenery changes so fast that it makes your head spin; you start feeling as if the landscape were being peeled from the surface of your body, layer after layer—it was like having someone rub a scab that's still oozing bodily fluids, rub it over and over, you feel as if your epidermis is never going to get itself together again, nothing protects you from the outside air. A peculiar sort of combined sensitivity and dullness affects your outer layers.

"So what eventually happens is that the yakuza take over the club. The guys on fifteen—that's the channel I'm on— we're all pretty friendly, but, man, over on channel six— they're fighting all the time. Most of the guys using six are real yakuza. You've got guys driving around while they're high on speed and stuff, you know; lots of really freaky handles, Speedy Gonzales and so on." "Ha ha, that's good. What about police radios and stuff, can you listen in on them?"

I kept talking. For some reason the idea that the conversation might end really frightened me. I was afraid of the feeling that always came over me at the moment that we stopped talking, the sense that the border between me and the night was gone. When I was a kid I had trouble telling the difference between sleep and death, so I was always afraid of the night.

"You can't get a police radio. Though, as a matter of fact, I did swipe one out of a police car back in my gang days. I sold it and one of those police lights to a guy in some right-wing organization." "A right-winger, huh?" "What do you say, do you think it's about time to hit the sack?"

I could see the lights on the other side of Tokyo

Bay. Okabe went back into the sleeper and I followed. Someone once told me why it is that in warmer winters you get a lot of snow, even at comparatively low altitudes, but I could no longer remember the reason why. Considering how warm it had been this winter, spring certainly seemed to be taking its time arriving. The lights over on the other side of the bay looked like a substance that the cold had caused to condense in mid-air. Okabe closed the middle curtain and the lights disappeared from view.

"Is this thing recording? I'm gonna stop it, OK?"

The REC button on the tape-recorder popped up. It felt as if something, a long ribbon that tied me to my past and my future, had suddenly snapped. The darkness of the night felt heavier. The perimeter of my being had shrunk. One by one the elements that comprised my world were being removed. Being, my being, was dwindling to the size of a head of a pin. Okabe narrowed the distance between us. Okabe seemed to be no one I knew. With every passing moment the portion of him that was made up of memory was slipping away; it was happening with him, too. I was unable to move. It struck me that if he hit me now, I would immediately tell him I was sorry and beg him to forgive me, et cetera—that I would simply accept it. Why am I thinking these stupid things, I thought, but even so I kept thinking them. Once again I found myself looking up to inspect the lock on the door.

Without saying a word, Okabe folded my head in

his arms. The instant before his hands embraced
me, his palms shifted to echo the subtle curves of my
skull—they rested perfectly, naturally, against me.
He was so extremely close, in a flash he made the air
turn sweet. He peeled the clothes from my lower
body.

"You do it."

Just as he'd said, I began caressing myself, and
soon I started secreting fluids, and little by little the
rough feeling started to fade away, like a hide being
tanned. The warm fluids kept oozing out, it was so
much more than I'd thought, so much that even my
anus was wet. His fingers began probing my anus.
For one very brief moment the muscles tensed,
hardening.

"Your asshole's twitching."

It was embarrassing enough just to have him say
this, but his timing was so exquisitely wrong that the
energy drained from my body. I don't like having
people feel my anus, not even people I'm going out
with—it's too much. But now it was coated in a
layer of fluid, it felt as if that coating were protecting it from harm. I didn't have the sense that it was
being touched directly, not at all, and the concept
of dirtiness never even entered my mind. His fingers
slipped lightly across the thick smokescreen of liquid
that concealed my anus. He slid his fingers halfway,
just halfway, up into my vagina, then started slipping
them in and out. He moved very slowly. The doorway
to my body clung to his fingers like a tropical fish

sucking on its food. Every so often the fingers that weren't inside brushed my anus. When that happened the sensations in my abdomen deepened even more. The entrance and the exit were moving on their own, doing things that embarrassed me. I had no idea what was being done to me, or where. The fluid kept flowing. I continued fingering my clitoris. I arrived at a small peak, and a spasm racked my body.

In the darkness there is an invisible attractant, and it is sucking me out. When I've been completely sucked out, I encounter Okabe's tip.

I had always thought having sex with a lover was like chatting. Chatting by means of your body. But this felt more direct—as if I were absorbing him directly. I used my fluids to suck him in; not just his penis but all of him; I was eating him. The mucous membrane coating my vagina had been reversed and now it was my whole body, obverse and reverse, it was extremely sensitive and timid yet at the same time avaricious. The softest part of the core within me emerged, and the truck made it feel even more defenseless. The surface of my body was trembling, shivering, the movements were so small you couldn't even see them happening, and I was ready to shriek, I felt an urge to cry out, and the only way I knew to calm myself was to suck in more skin, more mucus.

Okabe was entering me from behind. The darkness was bearing down on me. He had pushed up into me from the rear, and now I had the feeling that my clitoris was ejaculating. At the same time I felt something, a lump of something moving up into my throat—it was like when I force myself to vomit. The motion became a dry orgasm, climaxing between my eyebrows in an explosion of pure white.

I seemed to hear the roar of waves.

The engine was still idling.

When I woke the next morning, the warehouse district was starting to come alive. Here and there, trucks and forklifts were on the move. I heard the electric whine of a vehicle in reverse. Okabe moved the truck; at eight-thirty the unloading began. Moved the truck again at nine-twenty. Things we ate and drank: a packed lunch with rice and other things from a convenience store; hot coffee from a can.

We drove for a while after the loading finished, then towards evening we went to bathe. Almost all the gas stations that say they're "Designated Usami Stations" have baths. Usami is a group that made it big by targeting long-haulers—they've got places all over the country where you can bring in your truck, and they've all got baths. Regular cars hold about ten to thirteen gallons of gas; it takes about fifty-five to fill up the two tanks in a four-ton truck, so the profit is mutual. We filled up at the Usami on Route 17, then went for a bath. It was a nice bath, with a device attached outside that kept the water hot for twenty-four hours a day.

On our second trip to Niigata I was able to enjoy

the scenery. Then a voice came out of the CB:

Watch out, they're heatin' a griddle up ahead.

Nice of whoever it was to warn us. "Griddles" are the weigh stations—they're called that because that's just what the truck scales look like: long metal griddles. Apparently this was the first time Okabe had spoken to the guy who tipped us off. Thanks to his kindness, Okabe—who was trans- porting eleven tons of freight in his four-ton truck— was able to skirt around the checkpoint. On the CB, information like that is referred to as "a report," and they do all the reports in truckerspeak, using special codes. People making these reports are given priority—even in crowded areas they're given access to the air-waves. Speed is the "S-meter," police on motorcycles are "Moon Mask Riders," patrol cars are "Pandas." When you hear the slang, you can always see where it originated. I don't sup- pose the words are really selected to prevent the meanings from leaking out; it's more that, because the information is so crucial, you've got to be able to talk quickly without having to worry about different ways of saying things—that's why you need the slang.

"You wanna try talking?" asked Okabe after the report had come in and he had thanked the guy for making it. He offered me the mike. Maybe he figured I was getting bored now that night had fallen.

"Yeah, OK."

The smell of the shampoo we'd used had filled

the cab.

"Wanna pretend you're me?"

"What do you mean? How do I do that?"

"No one can tell who you are if you use this."

He handed me something black, about the same shape and size as the mike.

"What is it?"

"A voice converter. I'm not so hot on the things, but someone lent it to me and I still haven't got round to returning it."

"Isn't it kind of scary if you can't tell who it is?"

"They'll know by the handle. They'll just think I'm messing around. Don't worry, people do this all the time."

What's your handle again?

Storm.

The voices were back.

"Here, go ahead and talk."

He handed me the mike.

"Come in, this is Storm."

I pressed the transmit button on the mike. I held the voice converter between the mike and my mouth and spoke; there was a button that let you adjust the settings but I had no way of predicting how the effects would change my voice—*Come in, this is Storm.* The voice came from the outside. I heard my voice transformed into another that was thin and high and metallic.

I was no longer there.

Your voice changes. Mentally I should have been

prepared, I had known what was going to happen, and yet it made me feel sick. Hard goose pimples appeared on my skin. I suppressed a sudden urge to vomit, I sensed it coming on again, heard the click of something snapping back into place inside my head, like gears that have fallen out of sync coming together again. The voices were returning. They could say anything. It was like the very first time I heard a voice beyond my control—my own words transformed into a voice I didn't recognize at all.

"Hewow, hewow, howwah yuu?"

For some reason I found myself speaking baby-talk. I grasped the mike in my sweaty hands, holding down the button. I became conscious of the trembling of my hands. Then suddenly I realized what I was doing and took my thumb off the button it had been pressing. I glanced over at Okabe. He was facing forwards. There was a pause, then a response came from the person on the other end, but it was as if all the noise in the world had been absorbed by our single small speaker; it was impossible to separate out a single voice. Which voice should I respond to, I wondered, focusing so intently on the sound that it seemed as if the capillaries covering the surface of my head would all burst, but the whole world was being squeezed, transformed into nothing but a strange sound.

"It's like when gas is pressurized and turns into a liquid, like liquid propane?"

I hadn't meant to say this out loud, but I had.

I pressed the button and said, "Having trouble making you out."

Okabe reached out and grasped my hand, "The guy on the other end is still talking."

"Huh?"

I was picking up lots of voices in my head, as if any number of satellites had opened themselves up in there. Some of them sounded very far away.

"Do you hear a signal really far away?"

"No, I don't think so."

I found this awesome place in Kurosaki. Take me with you. *My name is* . . . OK then, we'll meet at the truck station. Hawaii, Hawaii. Man, that girl was beyond belief, going around spreading rumors like that, half of them not even true. Let me do it with your wife this time. What time? . . . n't, really. I'm telling you, I don't rent her out. Tango, Alpha, Queen, Queen. Eleven o'clock. Already. What the hell, you on the highway or something? What time did you say? And now it's time to take a look at some of the postcards we've received from . . .

I released the button and turned toward the driver's seat.

"Did you turn on the radio?"

"No."

But the radio is definitely talking. There are loads of people talking, and I'm sure I can hear the radio mixed in.

"Mind if I turn it on?"

"It's fine with me, but won't it be hard for you to

hear?"

"It's OK," I replied.

My mouth wasn't working. My head was turned slightly to one side, so there was nothing happening with the voice converter, but even so I could hear that unfamiliar, altered voice speaking along with my usual voice. I couldn't tell where the altered voice was coming from—it seemed to be speaking somewhere inside me, but it might also have been coming from the outside.

"There's a pause when you use the CB, right? I get sick of waiting."

Okabe didn't reply. I kept pressing the button on the digital tuner, changing wavelengths. Meaningful phrases drifted up one after another, electric whines and crackles mixed in between them.

This program has been brought to you by Fujitsu Computers . . . The contents of today's broadcast may be found on our web page. We've got all kinds of info there so I hope you'll take the time to check it out . . . Can I put it on AM? Sure. What did you say? Nothing, I just said you can if you want to. You want to listen to a CD? Nah . . . Well we just passed in the street and I fell for him / it's the first time that's ever happened to me / though I hear that it was love at first sight for my mom and dad / well he just took me away with him and then kicked me out / I'd been having trouble collecting my emotions for a while . . . we're in the middle of our Patty Page special. Patty was the second of eleven children. Her

famous "Tennessee Waltz" is . . . in most cases we
tend to assume that when the subjects are the same
a single person is being referred to, but in regions
where certain languages are spoken, as well as in the
worldview of infants and schizophrenics and so on,
it is more common to link people whose predicates
are the same because . . . oh, oh any slope at aaall /
having fuuun, so muuuch fuuun / it's so eaaaaasy . . .
Listen if that's what you're talking about, you want
the word "Spur," like in German, tracks on the
slope, slope would refer to the hill . . . thereupon
Buddhist Saint Shinran . . . this advertisement was
based on an e-mail from one of our office workers by
the name of Kitaura Kengo . . . Has it started raining?
No, it's the music. Now I'd like to introduce next
week's guest: we're going to have Kiyoharu from
Black Dream here and then the week after that we're
going to have the actress Inamori Izumi, and you
know the two of us are just like that, really, you
could say we're drinking buddies, yeah that's it,
drinking buddies is what we are, really, because we
go out drinking, though as a matter of fact we've
been out to eat a few times, too, and I've got to tell
you, I've got to tell you, she's such a darling, she
really is . . .

"Hey!"

I felt as if I'd bumped into an old friend.

I found it! I'm sure this is the voice I heard earlier!
A dialogue between a man and a woman. This is it
this is it this is it this is it. But could I really have

been hearing a radio that wasn't even on? A radio that *wasn't even on?* Of course, they weren't talking about the same stuff as before, time kept passing, so there was no way to see if it was true. These are different people, they're different from the ones who were talking earlier. I struggled to convince myself that this was the case. And then I realized that there were any number of different *mes* that existed simultaneously within the passing of time. I tried to feel the presence of the body of the *me* I was *here* and *now* but all I felt was a burning sensation on my skin; the inside was empty. Small holes began opening in the surface, and the holes kept multiplying, becoming more numerous; the gap between other people and myself was disappearing. Stop! Cover the skin, keep me from flowing out. Hold me hold me hold me, I'd plead with Okabe if I could, that's what I want, but it's too disconnected, so I hold it in. A flickering sensation is being fed directly to my nerves in the form of a pulse. My mouth tastes like a battery, sour and stimulating. The muscles in my arms twitched, movements in no way related to my volition. And as soon as they started twitching all the other muscles started contracting in waves; I had no idea what part of my body would be next. My teeth started chattering. There was a sound like something snapping—or so I thought until I understood that this wasn't a snapping sound at all: it was the sound of two things connecting.

I heard a voice.

Time to change clothes.

The waves in my muscles concentrated, swelled, rose like vomit.

Got to go to the gym next.

Mmm, replies a voice. The tone was different, but I could tell it was the same voice that had said *Time to change clothes.* It reminded me of an actress doing the voices for different characters in a cartoon, someone who does it really well. I felt a wave of nostalgia, tears nearly spilled from my eyes. I felt a wave of nostalgia so powerful it was frightening.

Put your arm in the sleeve.

Mmm.

Now all you have to do is straighten your arm.

Mmm.

The voices kept going back and forth, all on their own.

God, it just made me so angry, you know, that Yoshida guy, he's like totally going out with two girls at once, and he doesn't give a shit about how Kanako's gonna feel. Mmm. I figure it must be that guy on the basketball team, Ukai. Mmm. Now solve both those numbers into factors of X. Mmm. I mean, does that girl just make you totally sick or what? Mmm. Let's cut her.

Mmm mmm mmm mmm.

Uhhhhn, uhhhhhhhhhhhhhhhhhhhn—

I tried so hard to hold it in, but I hit the limit so fast it wasn't funny.

I'm gonna throw up.

Huh?

I'm gonna throw up.

Did you say something?

"I feel sick."

I pressed my hand to my mouth. I tried to look as if it were an emergency. What the hell are you saying girl, it *is* an emergency. Get off my back, what the hell good does it do to start needling yourself at a time like this, because it's true: this is a *real* emergency. This woman I'm friends with told me once that in emergency situations my voice sounds even calmer than usual. I hunched over, pressing my hand to my mouth. I had no choice but to act as though I were sick.

How could I have forgotten for so long?

Here, in this place, right now, a vague memory was being brought back to life: it occurred to me that maybe, just maybe, I'd started hearing those voices around the time I was in eighth grade. The voices hadn't come to harass me; the voices had come into being in order to protect me—I had created them myself. It wasn't as if I'd started hearing them all at once, either. I'd seen words falling to pieces. I stopped being able to conjugate the "ra-row" irregular verbs. Ever since that day when he'd hit me, that little bald man—that Japanese language teacher who didn't even speak proper Japanese, put "z"s in all sorts of places they didn't belong—ever since that day, once a day, no matter how hard I tried to put a barrier between us, he would call on me and make me stand. Even in home economics, when there wasn't the slightest need for anyone to give opinions on anything, he'd ask me what my opinion on something or other was and make me stand. He needed to have that sort of person, someone he could treat like that. And then one day he told me to repeat the "ra-row" irregular conjugations, even though I turned my head upside down looking for it, the passageway leading to the "ra-row" irregular conjugations wasn't there. I hadn't needed to think, I was conditioned so that it would appear when it was needed, but now I couldn't find it. I managed to reconstruct the circumstances under which I had said it before, but the characters where the conjugations ought to be were blanked out, nothing but perfectly white spaces. My voice wouldn't come. I opened and closed my mouth, but all I could do was suck in air, and in no time my lungs were filled. I went on sucking in air, because that was all I could do. My pulse quickened instantly. My field of vision shrank. The world retreated; I was overcome by the sense that a transparent membrane had formed, separating the world from me; no matter what I did, I couldn't touch it. That feeling of being unable to touch things that were right in front of me—it was like having the distance between me and the things in front of me subdivided into smaller and smaller units and then separated from me in temporal terms until the time confronting me was infinite. What will the teacher do? Will he hit me again? I can't touch

the world but he can invade my space from his side
no problem whatsoever. I had no choice but to drop.
My whole body went completely stiff, so I couldn't
manage a performance, a skillful stage fall; it hurt a
lot, but at least I was able to get out of that situation.
The teacher didn't do anything, but I was glad he
hadn't touched me. The two health monitors from
my class came and led me away, supporting me on
their shoulders. I hung from their shoulders like a
stick. There was no color in my face. Where had all
the blood in my body gone? I wanted to go on
enjoying the softness and warmth of their flesh forever, that was all I wanted. One of them was a boy,
one was a girl. Mochizuki and Hihara. They went
away very soon and that made me sad. I'd wanted to
go on tasting the different types of pleasure I felt in
the touch of male and female flesh. There was a
point of view, somewhere above them, from which I
gazed down at their departing backs. The linoleum
floor. A pale orange flight of stairs with little fragments of rock in the steps. School shoes. I was told,
as I lay in the nurse's office, that I had pubescent
anemia.

"I saw words falling to pieces."

The next day my mother asked me why I wasn't
going to school, and there were only two things I
could tell her. This time the broken passageway
yielded only two responses, as if they had been
imprinted on my mind. I lay trembling in my bed.
My body was composed of involuntary muscle

spasms. Gently, softly, my mother questioned me. As softly and as gently as she had been with me when I was a child sick with a cold.

"A psychiatrist."

"I want to go," I said, "to a psychiatrist." And in an instant the warm, pleasant aura that had hung in the air around my mother vanished. Then, after a few days, she came out with the suggestion that if I really didn't want to go to this school, perhaps I should move to another one. "This isn't doing you any good either, you know. And, you see, it makes us look so bad. We can go and have you registered as a resident at your grandfather's house, OK, that way you . . ." In those days, my grandfather's house was up to the north of Iwaki city. I did what my mother said: I went to take a look at the school. Gazing out of the train window on the way, I saw little points of yellow mixed in with the green of the fields, and then at certain places the points would suddenly gather into a cluster. Rape blossoms blooming in profusion. That's what they were. I began feeling a dim sense of excitement. But when we arrived nearer my grandfather's house the flowers were still closed in tight, green buds. It was already May, but it was cold there. Or maybe it was just cold that year; I don't know. I heard my mother mutter a few words, as if to herself: "Whose fault is it that we have to come out here to the backwoods?"

It's yours.

There's no doubt in my mind that I'd be able to

return an answer like that now, but at the time I didn't think of it, and the words didn't come. Which is more important to you, huh, your daughter or the school? Who the hell are you trying to protect? Back then I just felt what they told me to feel—I felt guilty. No matter how awful things were, I had to go back to school. My mother had no understanding of what it meant for words to fall apart. She didn't see how terrifying it was, not one bit, so she was trying to do something that would push me into an even more destructive terror. The only reason I was able to survive without words was that the people around me knew me. They shared my memories, helped me carry them, so even though I had stopped saying new things, I didn't disappear. If I remained silent in this entirely new environment, I would be beneath the threshold of existence, nothing but flesh, less than flesh. This time my words really would be lost. Going off to an unfamiliar environment was the one thing I absolutely couldn't do, the single thing I had to avoid at all costs.

I went back to the high school I'd originally attended and struggled desperately to listen to what people were saying. I listened so intently I felt like throwing up. My uniform looked no different from before, but underneath there was a place like a hole, and that hole was me. I'd draw people's words into that hole and then cut them up and paste them back together. I figured that since these were things people were saying, other people must be able to understand them. So I listened. And I tried to say things, to say what other people said. Of course, I couldn't just repeat the words someone standing right in front of me had said, so I'd create a file for them in my memory and save them and then use them in some other place, or at some other time. After that I learned to combine the things I had saved. All on my own, I arrived at an understanding of something like a grammar of the Japanese language. I realized that different meanings appear when you combine words in different ways. As infants we all do this unconsciously. I repeated the process in ninth grade. There were a few jerks who noticed the strange disjuncture between my seemingly unfazed face and the desperate struggle taking place inside me—they would come and bully me. I was disintegrating. The simple fact of existence made me disintegrate. Then, once I'd started going to school again, my parents gave me a warning: "Don't tell anyone that you were thinking of changing schools." Why not? "Well, it's certainly not going to help having people know, is it?" I got into the habit of examining my words before I spoke them. It takes a lot of concentration to swallow the words you were about to say and check them over again, and I wasn't at all sure I'd be able to continue to do it for long. So I made up my mind to act as if none of that stuff had ever happened. Nothing had happened. So I didn't remember anything. There was nothing, nothing had happened, so of course I didn't remember.

Then I heard the voices. The voices were a special kind of signal only I could understand, or rather they were a series of frequencies, and the thing was that I was the one transmitting them, just as I was the one receiving them. Once they were decoded, they turned into voices. That's how things had to work: if I did it any other way I was afraid the signals might be "intercepted" by other people, the way you intercept other channels on a CB. The wireless radio we call a CB uses an analog signal; it turns voices into waves and sends them flying out in that form, just as they are. But the radios used in police cars and fire engines and other more secretive radio systems have been digitized. They begin by changing the voice into a signal made up of 0s and 1s, then communicate with that. The "voices" I used were sort of like that, like a digital radio. The only difference was that my system was totally unique—I didn't share it with *anyone*. I couldn't let anyone else know. I even hid the mechanism from myself: I started thinking the voices had emerged from somewhere I was unaware of, that they had come to guide me. This can't be my own heart—it isn't.

"Hold on a sec." Okabe seemed flustered.

I was overjoyed to have this experience of moving the world. There are a lot of trucks out on all-night drives on the highways, and they drive pretty fast, so it's hard for any single truck to slow down.

"It was so sudden."

The indicator was flashing.

"I don't know what happened."

It makes me happy that I can do this, that the words I say and my attitude are enough to make a person become so flustered. Come on, girl, that's like a child thinking she's omnipotent, no? Wake up and smell the coffee: you're thirty-one!

"I'm gonna throw up. I'm gonna throw up."

"Sorry, I started feeling sick all of a sudden so I'm gonna stop now," he said in his normal voice, the mike in his hand, then whistled. He said the same thing in the same way to one other person, then whistled in the same way.

"What was that?"

What was that? Do it again!

"I cut off the communication."

"By whistling?"

"There are a bunch of fixed ways to cut things off. That way the person on the other end doesn't get worried even if you cut off suddenly."

I continued to feel kind of queasy. And yet there was still this place in me that felt strangely aroused, and since my ability to control it had long since slipped out of joint the desire wasn't stopping. In the layer of my brain that handled my memories, there was a group of cells that turned to look back at a whistle, and they were responding now. Whistle again for me—do me right here, right now. The cells in me that feel sexual desire were swelling, turning red, spurring me on.

We pulled onto the hard shoulder. I went outside, but my sense of balance had gone. Totter totter totter totter. I couldn't even vomit. Nothing came out but sour saliva, and I felt blood flowing into my eyes. I pushed my fingers back into my throat, but I still couldn't vomit. I used to be so good at this. There's a voice in my head that just keeps chitter-chatter-chitter-chattering, I can't manage to follow what it's saying; it's weird not being able to make out things that are happening in my own head. Chitter-chatter-chitter-chatter-chitter-chatter-chitter-chatter-chitter-chatter-chitter-chatter. You get so irritated when you want to vomit but you can't that all your hair stands on end, all over your body. You watch whoever you're with, noticing everything, even how he disturbs the air around him, and you automatically switch into fight mode. Even if it's a man you like, he gets on your nerves, and you get angry.

Don't touch me!

I swung my hand in a wide sweep. Okabe said, "Sorry," and jerked his hand back. I'm feeling extremely sensitive right now so please don't touch me. The words and the gestures were in my head, that option was there, but I couldn't get them out; I'm sorry I really want to be more gentle. When I'm having trouble throwing up the core of my body stiffens. I feel awful, so awful. I beat my fists against Okabe's chest. His soft, thick, elastic chest. I started feeling numb all the way from my fists to my elbows. It feels so good, so good. I want to hit him again. I hit him. I ram him with my head. Okabe doesn't respond the way he should, by showing pain. Once again. It seems like he may succeed in restraining my fists. I twist and turn, trying to break free. Don't touch me, don't touch me, please don't touch me. Otherwise I'll have to hit you.

When I realized I couldn't hit him, I began punching my own head.

Okabe seized my wrists but I struggled and finally managed to pull away, then I finally managed to vomit. The violent impulse I had felt settled down once I had vomited, but then I was seized by lethargy. This wasn't at all like throwing up after eating too much.

Okabe put me back in the truck, and we drove for a while, nice and slowly. At the first turn-off from the highway, Okabe stopped the truck.

He took out the key.

He led me by the hand; we walked; we went to a love hotel.

No matter where you went in the hotel it was dimly lit, and I was able to relax. There was no strong stimulus, nothing to grate on the nerves. It was the first time I had ever felt such gentleness in a love hotel. Once we were in the room, Okabe filled the bathtub with water, slightly warmer than body temperature.

How can this man know me so well?

The surface of my skin was feeling very sensitive; it couldn't tolerate any strong stimulation. Hot water would be no good; nor would a shower. I wanted to

be shielded from stimulation, wrapped in something, protected. Even Okabe's skin wasn't enough;
the little hairs on my body were all standing on end;
I wanted someone to soothe them. I wanted someone to make them lie down, make them all flat again,
like velvet rubbed the wrong way when you smooth
it down.

The vomit clinging to my neck and chest was
quietly washed away, not by the shower nozzle, but
with water scooped up in the container provided.
Then I was lowered into the tub. You think at some
point he might have been gentle with the stalker,
too? The voices started talking. It's not emotion that
make him gentle; it's instinct. He can be gentle even
when he feels no emotion; he can be gentle when
touching something soft. The way you're careful
when you touch a peach. My shoulders are out of the
water; they're cold. Just like an animal. Instinct,
instinct. But even some guys, you know, there are
guys who don't care if they're hurting the peach,
guys who think the peach is theirs. This guy's not
bad, is he? If I could be in the truck all the time, I'd
keep this one for myself, keep him to myself. If I fell
in love with him, I'd cry. You're such a moron. So
what if the man's got "a wife"—whatever, as if that
matters. You're in love? Divided, not coexisting.

I buried my face in the water, trying to cut off the
voices. Okabe seized my hair and pulled my face
back out again.

I wish he'd hold it down.

Again and again I tried to sink. Again and again Okabe pulled me up, shook his head from side to side. I lowered my eyes, kept myself from looking.

Submerge me.

This is all wrong. But I can't even stop myself. I want to be stopped. I want to be stopped. No one in the world but him can stop me, because I've never let anyone see. I hate myself when I'm like this, I hate myself but I'm alive.

"Beat me."

I squeeze this one desire into speech.

"Why?"

I want you to beat down the me in me that can't coexist with me.

Just beat me beat me beat me like you beat the stalker.

An ultrasonic scream, not a voice, filled the long, tiled, navy-blue bathroom.

Beat me — I was turned on by the word "beat." I was turned on by the arm that had beaten others in the past. Arms that punched and broke out of whatever situation, but went no further than that: they wouldn't kill. I wanted to hold tight to those arms, be protected by those arms. I was turned on by the memory of the things those arms had destroyed. I was turned on by those arms that no longer broke, that carried things with care.

"I can't beat you," Okabe replied. "I like you. I can't beat you."

Man, I don't know what you're talking about.

There in the warm water, as he rubbed my back, I cried. Several times I found myself overwhelmed by a sudden urge to vomit, but I couldn't; all I could do was cough. My body was buoyant, it rose in the water. Okabe hugged me to him, rubbed my back. And as he embraced me, as I cried, I had a feeling in my chest that I might, for whatever reason, call Okabe Mother.

Man, I just don't understand you at all.

Who's you? Okabe? Or yourself?

There's a voice. I don't know whose it is. Or if the voices like me or hate me. Or if they no longer exist purely to protect me, or when they changed.

Hey hey, you old bastard, what the hell are you doing?

Fine flakes of snow were streaming down.

You got me right on your ass like this and you still don't get it?

A perfectly straight, two-lane highway. The hatchback in front of us moves over to the left, lets the truck have the road.

Man, if you knew I was here you should've done that in the beginning.

With nothing before us, the sides of the road ahead suddenly cut in towards us. A narrow, high bridge came into view, stuck between two steep mountains. I'm seeing a line of yellow points. A cloud of snow blew up and across the ground. Those bits of yellow hovering there in the middle of all the

snow were like flowers on the bridge, blooming out
of season. As we approached we started to see legs,
and it turned into a line of kids walking home from
primary school, heading up the road. They were all
wearing dark yellow hats, so dark that when we got
nearer they looked closer to orange than yellow. I
guess when the visibility is bad they wear those
things on their way to and from school. There was
no pavement on the bridge. And when a car went by,
even a normal car, there was hardly any space left on
either side.

Okabe decreased speed as we drove onto the
bridge, then started heading over to the right to
open a space between the truck and the kids.
Another giant truck had stopped at the other end of
the bridge and was waiting there for Okabe to cross.
I stared down at the children's backs. Every so often
they would lose their footing in the snow. It looked
very dangerous.

I can't believe they're walking in this. Watch out
kids, huh?

Just then the last child in line turned around. I
froze. The child just stood there, gazing at our truck
as it approached, moving forward so slowly, and the
line of children left her behind. She looked up into
the truck, right into my eyes.

"Sure are quiet, aren't you?"

The child and Okabe and I all came together. I
didn't open my mouth. I simply made a noise,
shaking my head: *nnnnnn nnnnnn.* I haven't even

been saying that much, I've hardly spoken all along. I just drew you out.

"Are you tired?"

I made a noise that meant no and shook my head.

I saw where the snow ended. It was certain, I saw the point beyond which not a single snowflake would fall. The sun shone down instead, immediately causing the water to evaporate from the earth, making the landscape tremble. In the brilliant white of the truck, I felt stained with self-hatred and humiliation, and I said nothing.

The Shinano and Uono rivers had been running parallel to the truck, going off to the right and then over to the left again, but somewhere along the way they had stopped. Once we crossed the border and made our way into Gunma prefecture, all but a few of the ski resorts that had covered the mountains leading up to Mikuni Pass vanished. We drove on for a while. A lake appeared off to the right. I dimly recalled having heard that it was artificial. The surface of the lake was white and mushy—it had turned to slush. From time to time Okabe would say something to himself, things that required no response. "Man is it bright." "Gimme a break, you call this a highway?" Looking at a family restaurant: "Morning coffee for Dad." He'd probably say these things anyway, whether or not I was here. He said he liked me. But I'm just someone who butted into his life; maybe I'm fun to have around but maybe it'd be

no big deal if I were gone—is that all I was for him?
On the other hand, is it possible that having met
him won't change *me* at all? All these little moments
of release pile up, but then something just as small
pulls me back into the *me* I was before. I just kept
sitting there, silent.

The indicator was blinking. I heard the tires bite
into gravel. The truck came to a halt in a lot that
bulged out at the side of the road. We were at a
small restaurant with a parking lot for trucks. The
specials were written on the sign outside. I figured
maybe we were going to eat, but I didn't ask him
anything.

Then Okabe spoke. "You wanna try driving?"

"You're joking."

"You have a license, right?"

"Yeah."

"You can drive up to four tons with a regular
license."

"What? Are you serious?"

"You can drive."

"No way! I can't drive this."

"You can do it. I'll stop you if there's a problem."

Without leaving the cab, we switched seats.

Beyond the curved glass, I saw the shoveled lot in
front of the restaurant, and beyond that an
untouched field of white and a forest opening out
into a vast panorama. Here and there the black earth
lay exposed, rich with the water it had absorbed, and

the air was heavy with the scent of steaming soil. Air warmed by the sun rose into the cold air above it, and where the blades of heat crossed spirals would flicker into view, just for a moment. I had started to get used to the scenery, but now it all looked new again. I pressed my foot on the clutch and started to shift into first.

"Put it into second," said Okabe. "Unless you're going up a pretty steep hill or carrying stuff, you start driving in second. That's because of the torque."

I shifted into second. I concentrated on Okabe's words.

"Press down on the accelerator."

The world seemed to rise slightly. I quickly took my foot off the accelerator.

"Just give it some gas. You're doing fine."

The truck moved. The tires kicked up gravel, then gripped the road beneath it and sent it backwards.

"Change up."

I put it into third. It was different from driving a car. I could feel the clutch disc coming into contact with the pressure plate directly below my feet. My body sensed that the truck's movements were connected to its own.

"Go up one more."

My sense of the truck's weight decreased.

"I'm gonna end up on the road."

I'd kept the accelerator at the same position ever

since the truck had started moving and I'd been
driving more or less straight. I had taken us right
back to Route 17. The road continued. The truck
moved forwards. I felt as if my body had been
enlarged. The wheels turned, making noise. It was
the same noise they always made, but now it sounded
like a giant roar. The scenery wound back behind
me, brushing across my skin.

"Put it in there. Keep in mind how wide the turn
is and try to keep it nice and clean."

I looked where he was pointing and saw a snow-
plow station. The snowplows were all lined up
neatly in the corner of the lot. The road still continued. How am I supposed to know how wide the
turn is? My body can't feel the size of the truck.
But I tried to show him that I had things under
control, I tried to flick on the indicator, and then a
light force slowed the engine, and we were pulled
forwards.

"That's the exhaust brake."

I had moved the lever on the left of the steering
wheel. The indicator was on the right. The exhaust
brake works in pretty much the same way as the
engine brake. When I put it back in its original position, the brake came off very smoothly. Come to
think of it, that's what that special noise is that
trucks make when they're moving, that noise like
they're releasing air—that's the exhaust brake. They
must have this sort of thing because the clutch in a
truck is so heavy; that way you can get by without

having to change gear so frequently.

"Start turning right. Turn. Keep turning. Do just as I say."

The driver's side was now over the center line.

"A little more to the right. Change down. Now brake a little. Start turning left when you get over there."

I started turning left at the place Okabe had pointed to. The scenery streamed over to the right. The steering wheel had seemed to turn very easily when Okabe was driving, but it was a lot harder than it looked. I had trouble getting it to move. I realized that the wheels were caught in their own ruts. They weren't that deep, but they took control of the truck.

"More to the left, just keep turning left. Keep the accelerator where it is. OK, yeah, seems like you're making just about the tightest curve possible."

When I was actually turning the wheel, it didn't seem like it was necessary to turn back so much and make the truck balloon outwards like this, and it was hard to believe this was the tightest curve possible, but as those rear wheels started drawing closer to the corner I saw that they were really just barely making it past. Everything happens just as Okabe says. Everything that is supposed to happen happens, in the order it's supposed to happen.

"Wow! Oh wow!"

Once the truck had finished the turn, the landscape before us sat there, perfectly still, like an image on a screen.

"Turn the wheel back around."

Again the world spins.

"Well, you want to drive us back?"

Okabe sniffed, laughing. He's laughing at me because I feel like I already know how to drive this thing. The way he laughed made me feel as if he were someone I'd known for a very long time, and it felt good. Suddenly it occurred to me that when we went back to Tokyo this time, I'd go home. I didn't cry. Just over two hundred miles from Tokyo to Niigata, we'd gone round trip and then a little more than halfway through a second round-trip, six hundred miles and then a few more. The inside of my head cleared—I felt totally awake. All of the voices except for my main stream of thought had disappeared. I'll probably hear them again some day, but I'll deal with it; there's nothing else I can do but deal with it. But, for now, they've gone. I felt only the vibrations. I lifted my foot off the clutch. I noticed my own two hands, holding the steering wheel. I raised my thumbs. The nails weren't split any more. The thin layers of skin at the top had peeled off several times, and I could see the structures of new life underneath, pink and tense with energy, shallow fingerprints already carved into the skin. Various parts of me had absorbed water, I had reversed my mucous membranes, I had turned my whole body into pores, I had used my entire body to absorb this man, I had eaten him, every part of my body had been licked, my whole body had been absorbed and eaten. That's all this had been. It had no meaning.

But I felt as if I had become something good.

And that was enough.

Mari Akasaka lives in Japan. Winner of theNoma Literature Prize for best new writer in 2000, she is the author of three novels, of which the highly acclaimed Vibrator was made into a film in 2003.

Michael Emmerich is the translator of ten books, including Yasunari Kawabata's First Snow on Fuji; Genichiro Takahashi's Sayanara, Gangsters; and Banana Yoshimoto's Asleep.

CPSIA information can be obtained
at www.ICGtesting.com
Printed in the USA
LVHW040444070722
722903LV00004B/328

9 781933 368610